PR...
DICK FRANCIS AND
HIS PREVIOUS
THRILLERS

"Nobody sets up a mystery better than Dick Francis."

San Francisco Chronicle

"Francis captures our attention and holds us spellbound. . . . All the breathless pace we have come to expect of this superb writer."

The New York Times Book Review

"[Francis] has the uncanny ability to turn out simply plotted yet charmingly addictive mysteries."

The Wall Street Journal

With a New Introduction by the Author

KNOCKDOWN

Dick Francis

FAWCETT CREST • NEW YORK

A Fawcett Crest Book
Published by Ballantine Books
Introduction copyright © 1993 by Dick Francis
Copyright © 1974 by Dick Francis

Library of Congress Catalog Card Number: 74-15870

ISBN 0-449-22113-X

This edition published by arrangement with HarperCollins Publishers, Inc.

Manufactured in the United States of America

First Ballantine Books Edition: April 1993

11 10 9 8 7 6 5 4 3

Introduction

At Newmarket horse sales one October, a friend told me that all bloodstock agents were crooks. I listened rather vaguely to the catalogue of accusations, learning about the price-fixing rings and the blackmailing extortions which drove the sale prices of thoroughbreds up and down artificially.

In January, casting about belatedly for the core of a novel I ought already to have started, I remembered my friend's cynical indignation and sought her out, paying concentrated attention, this time, to the various scams she revealed.

Fortuitously I then heard of a small package tour being organized to fly British and Irish racehorse owners and bloodstock agents to the week-long bloodstock sales at Hialeah, Florida. Without hesitation I added my wife's and my name to the list, and we set out in a party of about twenty to spend glorious days by the sea in the sun and fascinating warm evenings watching the glossy horses sold under bright lights.

We listened and asked questions, our eyebrows rising to the hairline as even the bloodstock agents themselves told us how to cheat the bloodstock breeders out of a fortune.

We returned to February snow and, very late but at last, I invented my ex-jockey honest bloodstock agent, Jonah Dereham, thrusting him into a series of violent confrontations with a racketeering pack determined to force him to be as corrupt as themselves. Good versus evil in pretty basic terms!

In the recognition that no individual life is without sadness and tribulations, I often give my chief characters experiences of shadows and regrets. I burdened Jonah Dereham with an alcoholic brother to whom he felt tied by an exasperated but immutable love, and I made this brother a working cog in the plot so that he was not there simply to embarrass.

I like self-reliant women who don't need to bang a feminist drum. I gave Jonah Dereham a silver-cool woman and waited to see, as I went along, how the relationship would work out. It's always more interesting, to me, not to know every single outcome of my stories too far in advance.

Of course my Newmarket sales friend got it wrong, and of course she wildly exaggerated: not all bloodstock agents are crooks. The central message of *Knockdown*, however, is still valid and clear . . . *Caveat emptor*—BUYER BEWARE.

1

£

Mrs. Kerry Sanders looked like no Angel of Death.

Mrs. Kerry Sanders looked like a rich cross American lady opening a transparent umbrella against a spatter of cold rain.

"This," she said in disbelief, "is *Ascot* goddam *Sales*?"

She was small and exquisitely packaged in suède with mink trimmings. Her skin put peaches to rout and her scent easily prevailed over British October weather and a hundred nearby horses. With forty years behind her, she wore assurance as naturally as diamonds; and she wore diamonds like crusty knuckle-dusters across the base of all her fingers.

"*Ascot?*" she said, her voice brimming with overtones of

1

silk hats, champagne, and Royal Lawns. "This depressing dump?"

"I did try to warn you," I said with mild apology.

She gave me a sharp unfriendly glance. "You didn't say it was like something out of Dickens."

I looked across at the primitive sale ring: eight meters in diameter, open to the skies. A patch of rough field grass in the center encircled by an asphalt path for the horses to walk on, and surrounding that, for the comfort of the customers, an elementary wooden shelter, backed and roofed with planks.

Plans for a bright new tomorrow were already past the drawing board stage, but on that day the future warm brick building with civilized armchairs was still a twinkle in the architect's eye. The only available seating was a six-inch-wide wooden shelf running round the inside wall of the shelter at hip height, upon which few people ever rested for long owing to the local numbness it induced.

Throughout the sale ring's wooden O, the wind whistled with enthusiasm, but it was just possible when it was raining to find dry patches if you beat everyone else to them first.

"It used to be worse," I said.

"Impossible."

"There used to be no shelter at all."

She diagnosed the amusement in my voice and, if anything, it made her more annoyed.

"It's all very well for you. You're used to a rough life."

"Yes. . . . Well," I said, "do you want to see this horse?"

"Now that I'm here," she said grudgingly.

To one side of the sale ring, and built to a specification as Upstairs as the wooden circle was Downstairs, was a magnificent turn-of-the-century stable yard, paved and tidy, with rows of neat-doored boxes round a spacious quadrangle. There was intricate stone carving on the arches into the yard, and charming little ventilation turrets along the roofs, and Mrs. Kerry Sanders began to look more secure about the whole excursion.

The horses stabled in these prime quarters were in general those offered for sale last on the program. Unfortunately the horse she had insisted on inspecting before I bought it for her came earlier, and with a small sigh I wheeled her round in the opposite direction.

Thunderclouds immediately gathered again in the blue-green eyes, and two vertical lines appeared sharply between her eyebrows. Before her lay an expanse of scrubby wet grass with rows of functional black wooden stabling on the far side. The rain fell suddenly more heavily on the shiny umbrella, and the fine grained leather of her boots was staining dark and muddy round the edges.

"It's too much," she said.

I simply waited. She was there by her own choice, and I had used absolutely no pressure for or against.

"I guess I can see it in the ring," she said, which was no way to buy a horse. "How long before they sell it?"

"About an hour."

"Then let's get out of this goddam rain."

The alternative to the open air was the moderately new wooden building housing coffee urns at one end and a bar at the other. The Sanders nose wrinkled automatically at the press of damp humanity within, and I noticed, as one does when seeing through the eyes of visitors, that the board floor was scattered more liberally than usual with discarded plastic drinking cups and the wrappers from the sandwiches.

3

"Gin," Kerry Sanders said belligerently without waiting to be asked.

I gave her a brief meant-to-be-encouraging smile and joined the scrum to the bar. Someone slopped beer down my sleeve, and the man in front of me bought five assorted drinks and argued about his change: there had to be better ways, I thought resignedly, of passing Wednesday afternoons.

"Jonah," said a voice in my ear. "Not like you, chum, to chase the booze."

I glanced back to where Kerry Sanders sat at a small table looking disgusted. The eyes at my shoulder followed in her direction and the voice chuckled lewdly. "Some lay," he said.

"That chicken," I said, "is a customer."

"Oh, sure. Sure." The hasty retreat from offense, the placatory grin, the old-pals' slap on the shoulder—I disliked them all yet was aware they were only the desperate papering over no self-confidence. I had known him for years and we had jumped many a fence alongside: Jiminy Bell, one-time steeplechase jockey, currently drifting around horse places hoping for handouts. Where, but for the grace . . .

"Drink?" I suggested, and pitied the brightening eyes.

"Brandy," he said. "Large, if you could."

I gave him a treble and a fiver. He took both with the usual mix of shame and bravado, consoling himself inwardly with the conviction that I could afford it.

"What do you know of the Ten Trees Stud?" he asked, which was much like asking what one knew of the Bank of England. "I've been offered a job there."

If it had been a good job, he wouldn't be asking my opinion. I said, "What as?"

"Assistant." He made a face over the brandy, not from

4

the taste but from the realities of life. "Assistant stud groom," he said.

I paused. It wasn't much.

"Better than nothing, perhaps."

"Do you think so?" he asked earnestly.

"It's what you are," I said. "Not what you do."

He nodded gloomily, and I wondered if he was thinking, as I was, that it was really what you had *been* that mattered when you came face-to-face with the future. Without his ten years as a name in the sports pages, he would have settled happily for what he now saw as disgrace.

Through a gap in the crowd I saw Kerry Sanders staring at me crossly and tapping her fingers on the table.

"See you," I said to Jiminy Bell. "Let me know how you get on."

"Yeah."

I elbowed back to the lady. Gin and jollying softened the sales' impact and eventually she recovered some of the fizz with which she had set out from London in my car. We had come to buy a steeplechaser as a gift for a young man, and she had made it delicately clear that it was not the young man himself she was attached to, but his father. Premarital negotiations, I gathered, were in an advanced stage, but she had been reticent about names. She had been recommended to me, and me to her, by a mutual American acquaintance, a bloodstock agent called Pauli Teksa, and until two days earlier I had not known of her existence. Since then, she had filled my telephone.

"He will like it, don't you think?" she asked now for the seventh or eighth time, seeking admiration more than reassurance.

"It's a fantastic present," I said obligingly, and wondered

5

if the young man would accept it cynically or with joy. I hoped for her sake he would understand she wanted to please him more than bribe him, even if a bit of both.

"I think," I said, "that I ought to go over and take a quick look at the horse before it comes into the ring, just to make sure it hasn't bowed any tendons or grown any warts since I saw it last."

She glanced out at the rain. "I'll stay here."

"Right."

I squelched down to the drab old stables and found Box 126 with Lot 126 duly inside, shifting around on his straw and looking bored. Lot 126 was a five-year-old hurdler which someone with a macabre sense of humor had named Hearse Puller, and in a way one could see why. Glossy dark brown all over, he was slightly flashy-looking, holding his head high as if preening. All he needed was a black plume on his head and he'd have been fine for Victorian trips to the cemetery.

Kerry Sanders had stipulated that her gift should be a young good-looking past winner, with cast-iron future prospects. Also that in all its races it should never have fallen. Also that it should be of a caliber pleasing to the father even though it was to be given to the son. Also that it should be interesting, well-bred, sensible, brave, bursting with health, and keen to race—in short, the perfect chaser. Also that it should be bought by Friday, which was the young man's birthday. Also it should cost no more than six or seven thousand dollars.

That had been the gist of her first call to me on Monday afternoon. She had conceived the idea of the gift at two o'clock, found my name by two-ten, and talked to me by two-twenty. She saw no reason why I should not put the same

6

sort of hustle on, and seemed delighted when I suggested Ascot Sales. Which was, of course, before she went there.

No one buys the perfect novice steeplechaser for seven thousand dollars. Most of my time since Monday had been taken both by persuading her to settle for a 50 percent reduction on perfection and by searching through the Ascot catalogue for a cut-price paragon. I had come up finally with Hearse Puller, knowing that she would object to the name. It had no breeding to speak of but I had seen it race and knew it had guts, which was half the battle, and it was trained by a nervy trainer, which meant it might do better somewhere more relaxed.

I felt Hearse Puller's legs and peered at the tonsils, and went back and told Kerry Sanders that her money was on the way.

"You think we'll get him, then?" she asked.

"As long as no one else wants him very badly."

"Do you think they will?"

"Can't tell," I said, and wondered how many times every year I had this same conversation. Nothing warned me there was anything different this time.

The rain had slackened to drizzle by the time we went over to the ring, but even so it was difficult to find room for Kerry Sanders in a dry spot. No one in the raincoated assembly looked much except miserable. They stood with hunched shoulders, coat collars turned up, hands in pockets, the usual collection of bloodstock agents, racehorse trainers, breeders, and hopeful would-be purchasers all out on the same trail of winners and loot.

Lot 122, a sad-looking chestnut, plodded round the asphalt path and failed to reach his reserve—the price below which he could not be sold—despite the auctioneer's cajoling. I told Kerry Sanders I would be back in a minute, and went to watch 126 being led round in the collecting ring as he waited his turn. He carried himself well enough but he looked a little too excited, and I thought that the rain was probably hiding the fact that he was sweating.

"You interested in that black peacock?" said a voice at my shoulder, and there again was Jiminy Bell, following the direction of my eyes and giving me the benefit of the treble brandy at close quarters.

"Not specially," I said, and knew he couldn't have read anything from my face. Nothing like bloodstock dealing for encouraging an expression to make poker players look indiscreet.

Hearse Puller pranced past and I switched my attention to 127, coming along next.

"Now, that one," Jiminy said approvingly. "Bit of class there."

I grunted noncommittally and turned toward him. He made way for me with a half-aggressive half-ingratiating smile, a short man with graying hair, deeply wrinkled skin, and teeth too good to be true. Four or five years out of the saddle had put weight on him like a padded coat, and all his past pride in being able to do a job well had evaporated from his general carriage and the way he held his head. But, feel sorry for him as I might, I had no intention of telling him in advance in which direction my interest lay: he was well into the stage of trotting off with the news to the vendor and asking a commission for bidding the price up high.

"I'm waiting for number one four two," I said, and as soon as I walked off he started busily looking it up in the catalogue. When I glanced back, he was staring after me in amazement, so I looked up 142 out of curiosity and found it was a crib-biting point-to-pointer still a maiden at ten.

Laughing inwardly, I rejoined Kerry Sanders and watched the determined auctioneer wring twelve hundred pounds out of the U.K. Bloodstock Agency on the sinewy chestnut mare who was Lot 125. As she was led out, I felt Kerry Sanders stir beside me with her intentions showing to all and sundry like a flourish of trumpets. Inexperienced customers always did this if they came to the sales, and it cost them a good deal of money.

Hearse Puller was led into the ring and the auctioneer checked his number against his notes.

"Bit on the leg," a man behind us said disparagingly.

"Is that bad?" Kerry Sanders asked anxiously, overhearing.

"It means his legs are long in proportion to his body. It's not ideal, but some good chasers are like that."

"Oh."

Hearse Puller tossed his head and regarded the scene with eyes filled with alarm, a sign of waywardness that made me wonder if that was the basic reason for selling him.

Kerry Sander's anxiety grew a little.

"Do you think he'll be able to manage him?"

"Who?"

"His new owner, of course. He looks damn wild."

The auctioneer began his spiel, reeling off the gelding's origins and history. "Who'll start me at a thousand? A thousand anywhere? Come along, now; he'd look cheap at that, wouldn't he? A thousand? Well, five hundred, then. Someone start me at five hundred. . . ."

I said to Kerry Sanders, "Do you mean the young man is going to ride him himself? In races?"

"Yes."

"You didn't tell me that."

"Didn't I?" She knew she hadn't.

"Why didn't you, for heaven's sake?"

"Five hundred," said the auctioneer. "Thank you, sir. Five hundred I have. That's nowhere near his value. Come along, now. Five hundred. Six. Thank you, sir. Six . . . Seven . . . Eight . . . against you, sir. . . ."

"I just—" She hesitated, then said, "What difference does it make?"

"Is he an amateur?"

She nodded. "But he's got what it takes."

Hearse Puller was no armchair ride and I would be doing my job badly if I bought him for the sort of amateur who bumped around half fit. The customer's insistence on the horse never having fallen suddenly made a lot of sense.

"Twelve hundred. Fourteen. Against you at the back, sir. Fourteen. Come along, now, you're losing him. . . ."

"You'll have to tell me who it's for," I said.

She shook her head.

"If you don't, I won't buy it for you," I said, trying with a smile to take the discourtesy out of the words.

She stared at me. "I can buy it myself."

"Of course."

The auctioneer was warming up. "Eighteen . . . can I make it two thousand? Two thousand—thank you, sir. Selling all the time now. Two thousand . . . against you in front. . . . Shall I say two thousand two? Two thousand one. . . . Thank you, sir. Two thousand one . . . two . . . three . . ."

"It will be too late in a minute," I said.

She came to a decision. "Nicol Brevett, then."

"Jeez," I said.

"Buy it, then. Don't just stand there."

"All done?" said the auctioneer. "Selling at two thousand eight hundred. Selling once . . . all done, then?"

I took a breath and waved my catalogue.

"Three thousand . . . New bidder. Thank you, sir. . . . Against you in front. Can I make it three thousand two?"

As often happens when a fresh bidder comes in at the last moment, the two contestants soon gave up, and the gavel came down at three thousand four.

"Sold to Jonah Dereham."

Jiminy Bell was staring at me slit-eyed from the other side of the ring.

"What's that in dollars?" said my client.

"About seven thousand five hundred."

We left the wooden shelter and she raised the umbrella again, although the drizzle had all but ceased.

"More than I authorized you to spend," she said, without great complaint. "And your commission on top, I guess?"

"Five percent," I said, nodding.

"Ah, well . . . In the States you wouldn't buy a three-legged polo pony for that money." She gave me a small smile as nicely judged as a tip, and decided to walk on to wait in my car while I completed the paperwork and arranged for the onward transport of Hearse Puller. He was to be stabled for the night in my own backyard and delivered to his new owner on the birthday morning.

Nicol Brevett . . . A surprise like a wasp at the honey, harmless unless you touched it on the stinging side.

He was a hard forceful young man who put his riding cards on the table and dared the professionals to trump them. His obsessive will to win led him into ruthlessness, rudeness, and rows. His temper flared like a flamethrower. No one could deny his talent, but where most of his colleagues won friends and races, Nicol Brevett just won races.

Hearse Puller was within his scope as a rider, and if I was lucky they would have a good season together in novice chases. And I thought I would need to be lucky because of Brevett, senior, whose weight could be felt all over the turf.

My respect for Kerry Sanders rose several notches. Any woman who could interest Constantine Brevett to the point of matrimony had to be of a sophistication to put Fabergé eggs to shame, and I could well understand her coyness about naming him. If any announcements concerning him were to be made, he would want to make them himself.

Constantine covered with velvet the granite core that showed in rocky outcrops in his son, and from brief race-course meetings over the past few years I knew his social manners to be concentrated essence of old-boy network. The actions that spoke truer had repeatedly left a wake of smaller operatives who sadly wished they had never been flattered by his attention. I didn't know exactly what his business was, only that he dealt in property and thought in millions, and was now trying to build up the best collection of horses in the country. I had guessed it was being best that interested him more than the actual horses.

When I was ready to leave the sales, the best thing of the day was due to come up in the ring, so it seemed that every-one was flocking in one direction to watch it while I went in the other toward the cars. I could see Kerry Sanders sitting waiting, her head turned toward me behind the rain-speckled glass. Two men were leaning on the car beside mine, cupping their hands over matches while they lit cigarettes.

When I passed them, one of them picked up some sort of

bar from the bonnet of the car and hit me a crunching blow on the head.

Dazed and astonished, I staggered and sagged and saw all those stars they print in comic strips. Vaguely I heard Kerry Sanders shouting and opening the door of my car, but when the world stopped whirling a little I saw that she was still sitting inside. Door shut, window open. Her expression as much outrage as fright.

One of the men clutched my right arm, which probably stopped me falling flat on my face. The other calmly stood and watched. I leaned against the car next to mine and weakly tried to make sense of it.

"Muggers," Kerry Sanders said scathingly. I thought she said "buggers," with which I agreed, but finally understood what she meant.

"Four pounds," I said. "Only got four pounds." It came out as a mumble. Indistinct.

"We don't want your money. We want your horse."

Dead silence. They shouldn't have hit my head so hard if they wanted sense.

Kerry Sanders made things no clearer. "I've already told you once that I intend to keep him," she said icily.

"You told us, but we don't believe you."

The one doing the talking was a large cheerful man with a bouncer's biceps and frizzy mouse-brown hair standing round his head like a halo.

"A fair profit I offered you," he said to Kerry. "Can't say fairer than that, now, can I, darlin'?"

"What the hell is going on?" I asked thickly.

"See, now," he said, ignoring me. "Three thousand six. Can't say fairer than that."

Kerry Sanders said no.

Frizzy Hair turned his reasonable smile on me.

"Look, now, lover boy, you and the lady is going to sell us the horse. Now we might as well do it civilized like. So give her some of your expensive advice and we'll be on our way."

"Buy some other horse," I said, still mumbling.

"We haven't got all afternoon, lover boy. Three thousand six. Take it."

"Or leave it," I said automatically.

Kerry Sanders almost laughed.

Frizzy Hair dug into an inner pocket and produced wads of cash. Peeling a few notes away from one packet, he threw the bulk of it through the car window onto Kerry Sanders's lap, followed by three closely taped packets that he didn't count. The lady promptly threw the whole lot out again, and it lay there in the mud of the car park, lucre getting suitably filthy.

The haze in my head began to clear and my buckling knees to straighten. Immediately, sensing the change, Frizzy Hair shed the friendly-persuader image in favor of extortionist, grade 1.

"Let's forget the games," he said. "I want that horse and I'm going to get it. See?"

He unzipped the front of my rainproof jacket.

I made a mild attempt at freeing myself from the other man's grasp, but my coordination was still shot to pieces. The net result was nothing except a fresh whirling sensation inside my skull, and I'd been knocked out often enough in the past to know that the time of profitable action was still a quarter of an hour ahead.

Under my jacket I wore a sweater, and under that a shirt. Frizzy Hair slid his hand up between these two layers until his fingers encountered the webbing strap I wore across my chest. He smiled with nasty satisfaction, yanked up the sweater, found the buckle on the strap, and undid it.

"Now you see, don't you, lover boy," he said, "how I'm going to get that horse?"

2

£

I sat in the driving seat of my car leaning my head against the window. Kerry Sanders sat beside me with the muddy packets of money on her expensive suède lap and unadulterated exasperation in her manner.

"Well, I couldn't just sit there and watch them putting you through a wringer," she said crossly. "Someone had to get you out of that fix, didn't they?"

I said nothing. She had stepped out of the car and picked up the money and told the thugs to leave me alone. She said they could have the goddam horse, and much good might it do them. She had not tried screaming for help or running away or anything equally constructive, but had acted on the great modern dictum that you became less of a hospital case if you gave in to threats of violence right away.

"You looked as gray as death," she said. "What did you expect me to do? Sit and applaud?"

I didn't answer.

"What's the matter with your goddam arm, anyway?"

"It dislocates," I said. "The shoulder dislocates."

"All the time?"

"Oh, no. Not often. Only if it gets into one certain position. Then it falls apart, which is very boring. I wear the strap to prevent that happening."

"It isn't dislocated now, is it?"

"No." I smiled involuntarily. I tended not to be able to sit comfortably in cars whenever it went out.

"Thanks to you," I added.

"As long as you realize."

"Mm."

They had taken the certificate of sale out of my pocket and had made Kerry Sanders write a receipt for the cash. Then they had simply walked away toward the center of operations to claim their prize. Kerry Sanders had not felt like trying to stop them and I had hardly been able to put one foot in front of the other with any certainty, and the one sure thing on that unsure afternoon was that Frizzy Hair and his pal would waste no time in driving off with Hearse Puller to destinations unknown. No one would question their right to the horse. Rapid post-sale sales were common.

"Why?" she said for the twentieth time. "*Why* did they want that goddam horse? Why *that* one?"

"I absolutely don't know."

She sat fidgeting.

17

"You said you'd be able to drive by four."

I glanced at the clock on the dashboard. Five past.

"Right." I removed my head from the window and gave it a small tentative shake. Reasonable order seemed to have returned in that department, so I started the engine and turned out toward London. She made a rapid assessment of my ability to drive and relaxed a shade after we had gone half a mile without hitting anything. At that point grievance took over from shock.

"I'm going to complain," she said with vigor.

"Good idea. Who to?"

"Who to?" She sounded surprised. "To the auctioneers, of course."

"They'll commiserate and do nothing."

"Of course they will. They'll have to."

I knew they wouldn't. I said so.

She turned to look at me. "The Jockey Club, then. The racing authorities."

"They have no control—no jurisdiction—over the sales."

"Who does, then?"

"No one."

Her voice sharpened with frustration. "We'll tell the police."

"If you like."

"The Ascot police?"

"All right."

So I stopped at the police station and we told our story. Statements were taken and signed, and no doubt filed as soon as we left, because as an overworked sergeant tiredly pointed out, we had not been robbed. A bang on the head, very nasty, very reprehensible, a lot of it about. But my wallet hadn't been stolen, had it? Not even my watch? And these rough customers had actually given Mrs. Sanders a *profit* of two hundred pounds. Where was the crime in that, might one ask?

We drove away, me in resignation, Kerry Sanders in a boiling fury.

"I will not be pushed around," she exploded. "Some-one—*someone* has got to do something."

"Mr. Brevett?" I suggested.

She gave me one of her sharp glances and noticeably cooled her voice.

"I don't want him bothered with this."

"No," I said.

We drove ten miles in thoughtful silence.

She said eventually, "Can you find me another horse by Friday?"

"I could try."

"Try, then."

"If I succeed, can you guarantee that no one else will knock me on the head and pinch it?"

"For a man who's supposed to be tough," she said, "you're soft."

This dampening opinion led to a further five miles of silence. Then she said, "You didn't know those two men, did you?"

"No."

"But they knew you. They knew about your shoulder."

"They did indeed."

"You'd thought of that, had you?" She sounded disappointed.

"Mm," I said.

I steered with care through the London traffic and stopped outside the Berkeley Hotel, where she was staying.

"Come in for a drink," she said. "You look as if you could use one."

"Er . . ."

"Aw, c'mon," she said. "I won't eat you."

I smiled. "All right."

Her suite looked out over Hyde Park, with groups of riding-school ponies trotting in the Row and knots of household cavalry practicing for state occasions. Late-afternoon sunshine slanted into the lilac-and-blue sitting room and made prisms of the ice cubes in our glasses.

She protested over my choice.

"Are you sure you want Perrier?" she said.

"I like it."

"When I said come up for a drink, I meant a *drink*."

"I'm thirsty," I said reasonably. "And a touch concussed. And I'm driving."

"Oh." Her manner changed subtly. "I understand," she said.

I sat down without being asked. It was all very well having had extensive experience of bangs on the head, but this had been the first for three years and the interval had not improved my speed of recovery.

She gave me a disillusioned glance and took off her beautiful muddied coat. Underneath she wore the sort of simplicity only the rich could afford on the sort of shape that was beyond price. She enjoyed my silent appreciation and took it naturally as the most commonplace courtesy.

"Now, look," she said. "You haven't said a goddam thing about what happened this afternoon. What I'd like is for you to tell me just what you think those men were up to back there."

I drank the fizzy water and fractionally shook my head.

"I don't know."

"But you must have ideas," she protested.

"No." I paused. "Did you tell anyone you were going to Ascot Sales? Did you mention me? Did you mention Hearse Puller?"

"Hey, now," she said. "It was you they were after, not me."

"How do we know?"

"Well . . . your shoulder."

"Your horse."

She moved restlessly across the room, threw the coat over a chair, and came back. The slim boots had dirty watermarks round the edges of the uppers that looked incongruous against the pale mauve carpet.

"I told maybe three people," she said. "Pauli Teksa was the first."

I nodded. Pauli Teksa was the American who had given Kerry Sanders my name.

"Pauli said you were an honest bloodstock agent and therefore as rare as fine Sundays."

"Thanks."

"Then," she said pensively, "I told the guy who fixes my hair."

"Who what?"

"Hairdresser," she said. "Right downstairs here in the hotel."

"Oh."

"And I had lunch with Madge yesterday . . . Lady Roscommon. Just a friend."

She sat down suddenly opposite in an armchair with a blue-and-white chintz cover. A large gin-and-French had brought sharp color to her cheeks and a lessening in her

21

slightly dictatorial manner. I had the impression that for the first time she was considering me as a man instead of as an employee who had fallen down (more or less literally) on the job.

"Do you want to take your coat off?" she asked.

"I can't stay," I said.

"Well, then . . . do you want more of that goddam water?"

"Please."

She refilled my glass, brought it back, sat down.

"Don't you ever drink?" she said.

"Not often."

"Alcoholic?" she said sympathetically.

I thought it odd of her to ask such a personal question, but I smiled and said, "No."

She raised her eyebrows. "Nearly all the nondrinkers I know are reformed alcoholics."

"I admire them," I said. "But no. I was hooked on Coke at six. Never graduated."

"Oh." She seemed to lose interest in me. She said, "I am on the committee of a private hospital back home."

"Which dries out drunks?"

She didn't care for the bluntness. "We treat people with a problem. Yes."

"Successfully?"

She sighed. "Some."

I stood up. "You can't win them all." I put the empty glass on a side table and went ahead of her to the door.

"You'll let me know if you find another horse?" she said.

I nodded.

"And if you have any thoughts about those two men?"

"Yes."

* * *

I drove slowly home and put the car in the garage in the stable yard. The three racehorses there moved around restlessly in their boxes, mutely complaining because I was two hours late with their evening feed. They were horses in transit, waiting to be shipped by air to foreign buyers—not my horses but very much my responsibility.

I talked to them and fondled their muzzles, and straightened their boxes and gave them food and water and rugs against the October night, and finally, tiredly, took my own throbbing head into the house.

There was no wife there waiting with a smiling face and a hot tempting dinner. There was, however, my brother.

His car was in the garage next to mine, and there were no lights anywhere in the house. I walked into the kitchen, flicked the switch, washed my hands under the hot tap in the sink, and wished with all my heart that I could off-load my drinking problem onto Kerry Sanders and her do-good hospital.

He was in the dark sitting room, snoring. Light revealed him lying facedown on the sofa with the empty Scotch bottle on the carpet near his dangling hand.

He didn't drink often. He tried very hard, and he was mostly the reason I stayed off it, because if I came home with alcohol on my breath he would smell it across the room, and it made him restless. It was no hardship for me, just a social nuisance, as Kerry Sanders was by no means alone in concluding that nondrinkers were ex-alcoholics. One had to drink to prove one wasn't, like natural bachelors making an effort with girls.

We were not twins, though much alike. He was a year older, an inch shorter, better-looking, and not so dark.

People had mistaken us for each other continually when we had been young, but less so now at thirty-four and thirty-five.

I picked up the empty bottle and took it out to the dustbin. Then I cooked some scrambled eggs and sat down at the kitchen table to eat, and over coffee and aspirin and a sore head put up a reasonable fight against depression.

There was much to be thankful for. I owned outright the house and stable yard and ten acres of paddocks, and after two years' slog I was beginning to make it as an agent. On the debit side I had a busted marriage, a brother who lived off my earnings because he couldn't keep a job, and a feeling that Frizzy Hair was only the tip of an iceberg.

I fetched a pen and a sheet of paper and wrote three names.

> Pauli Teksa
> Hairdresser
> Lady Roscommon (Madge)

None looked a winner in the villainy stakes.

For good measure I added Kerry Sanders, Nicol Brevett, Constantine Brevett, and two thugs. Shake that lot together and what did we get? A right little ambush by someone who knew my weakest spot.

I spent the evening trying by telephone to find a replacement for Hearse Puller. Not easy. Trainers with horses the owners might sell were not keen to lose them from their yards, and I could give no guarantee that Nicol Brevett would leave his horse with its present trainer. Bound by Kerry Sanders, I could not even mention his name.

I reread the Ascot Sales catalogue for the following day but there was still nothing suitable, and finally with a sigh I offered my custom to a bloodstock dealer called Ronnie North, who said he knew of a possible horse that he could get if I would play ball.

"How much?" I said.

"Five hundred."

He meant that he would sell me the horse for a price. I would then charge Kerry Sanders five hundred pounds more and hand the five hundred over to North.

"Too much," I said. "If you get me a good one for two thousand, I'll give you a hundred."

"Nuts."

"A hundred and fifty." I knew he would probably acquire the horse for maybe fifteen hundred pounds, and sell it to me for double; he always considered he had wasted his time if he made less than 100 percent profit. Squeezing a large chunk more from my client was just icing on the cake.

"And," I said, "before we go any further, I want to know about it."

"Do me a favor."

He was afraid that if I knew who owned the horse I would go direct to the source and cut him out altogether. I wouldn't have done that, but he would, and he judged me by himself.

I said, "If you buy it and I don't like it, I won't take it."

"It's what you want," he said. "You can trust me."

I could perhaps trust his judgment of a horse, though that was absolutely all. If the horse hadn't been for Nicol Brevett, I might have taken a chance and bought blind, but in this case I could not afford to.

"I have to O.K. it first."

"Then no deal," he said succinctly, and disconnected.

I chewed the end of my pencil and thought about the bloodstock jungle that I had entered with such innocence two years earlier. It had been naïve to imagine that all it took to be a bloodstock agent was a thorough knowledge of horses, an intimate relationship with the studbook, hundreds of acquaintances in the racing industry, and a reasonable head for business. Initial surprise at the fiddles I saw all around me had long since passed from revulsion to cynicism, and I had grown a thick skin of self-preservation. I thought that sometimes it was difficult to perceive the honest course, and more difficult still to stick to it, when what I saw as dishonesty was so much the general climate.

I understood, after two years, that dishonesty was much a matter of opinion. There were no absolutes. A deal I thought scandalous might seem eminently reasonable to others. Ronnie North saw nothing wrong at all in milking the market for every possible penny, and he was likable to meet in spite of that.

The telephone rang. I picked up the receiver.

"Jonah?"

He was back, as I'd thought he might be.

"The horse is River God. You can have it for three thousand five hundred with five hundred on top."

"I'll call you back."

I looked up the River God form and consulted a jockey who'd ridden it a few times, and finally dialed Ronnie North.

"All right," I said. "Subject to a vet's report, River God will do well."

He said with elaborate resignation, "I told you, you can trust me."

"Yeah. I'll give you two thousand five hundred."

"Three thousand," he said. "And that's rock bottom. With five hundred to come."

"One fifty," I said positively, and compromised at a hundred more.

River God, my jockey friend had said, belonged to a farmer in Devon who had bought it unbroken at three years old as a point-to-point prospect for his son. Between them they'd done a poor job of the breaking and now the son couldn't control the result. "He's a ride for a pro," said my informant, "but he's quite fast and a natural jumper, and they haven't managed to cock that up."

I rose, stretched, and, as it was by then half past ten, decided to tell Kerry Sanders in the morning. The room I used as an office, lined with bookshelves and filing cupboards, was half functional, half sitting room, and mostly what I thought of as home. It had a lightish brown carpet, red woolen curtains, leather armchairs, and one big window that looked out to the stable yard. When I had tidied away the books and papers I'd been using, I switched off the powerful desk lamp and stood by the window, looking out from darkness to moonlight.

Everything was quiet out there, the three lodgers patiently waiting for their airplane from Gatwick Airport, five miles down the road. They should have been gone a week since, and the overseas customers were sending irritable cables, but the shipping agents muttered on about unavoidable delays and kept saying the day after tomorrow.

"The day after tomorrow never comes," I said, but the agents didn't think it funny.

I used the yard as a staging post and seldom kept horses there more than a night or two. They were a tie, because I looked after them myself, and I did that because until recently I had not been earning enough to think of employing anyone else.

In my first year in the business I had negotiated fifty sales, in my second ninety-three, and during the past three months I had been almost constantly busy. Given a bit of luck, I thought—like, say, buying a Derby winner for five thousand as a yearling . . . just some such impossible bit of luck—I might yet achieve tax problems.

I left the office and went along to the sitting room. My brother Crispin was still where I'd left him, facedown, snoring, spark out. I fetched a rug and draped it over him, knowing he wouldn't wake for hours, and that when he did he would be in his usual violent hangover temper, spewing out his bitter resentments like untreated effluent.

We had been orphaned when I was sixteen and he seventeen, first by a riding accident that killed our mother, and then three months later by a blood clot in Father. Abruptly, almost from one week to the next, our lives changed to the roots. We had been brought up in comfort in a house in the country, with horses to ride and a cook and gardener and stablemen to do the work. We had gone to expensive boarding schools and had thought it natural, and holidayed on grouse moors in Scotland.

The glitter had by no means been founded on gold. Solicitors gravely told us that our parent had mortgaged all he possessed, had borrowed on his life insurance, had sold the family treasures, and was only a Degas sketch away from bankruptcy. He had, it appeared, been living on the brink of disaster for several years, always finding a last-minute goody to send to Sotheby's. When his debts had been paid and house, horses, cook, gardener, stablemen, and all had vanished into limbo, Crispin and I, without close relatives, were left with no home to go to and precisely one hundred and forty-three pounds each.

The school had been understanding but not to the point of keeping us without fees. We had finished the Easter term, but that was that.

It had affected Crispin more than me. He had been aiming for university and the law, and could not bring himself to settle for the generously offered articles of apprenticeship in the grave solicitor's office. My more practical nature saved me from such torments. I faced prosaically the fact that from now on I would need to work to eat, totted up my assets, which proved to be a thin body, good health, and a certain facility on horseback, and got myself a job as a stable lad.

Crispin had been furious with me but I'd been happy. I was not academic. Stable life, after the confines of school, had been a marvelous freedom. I never regretted what I'd lost.

I left him snoring and went upstairs to bed, thinking about our different fates. Crispin had tried stockbroking and insurance, and felt he had not been appreciated, and I, in becoming a jockey, had found total fulfillment. I always reckoned I'd had by far the best of it and didn't begrudge anything I could do to compensate.

My bedroom, like the office, looked out to the yard, and except when it was freezing I slept with the window open. At twelve-thirty I woke from the depths with the sudden instant awareness of the subconscious hitting the alarm switch.

I lay tinglingly awake, listening at full stretch, not knowing what I'd heard but sure that it was wrong.

Then, unmistakably, it came again. The scrape of a hoof

on a hard surface. The clop of horseshoes where they had no business to be at that time of night.

I flung back the bedclothes and jumped to the window.

No movement down there in the moonlit yard. Just a yawning black oblong that should have been filled by a firmly closed stable door.

I cursed with a sinking heart. The most valuable of my lodgers, all seventy thousand pounds' worth, was out loose on the dangerous roads of Surrey.

3

£

He wasn't comprehensively insured, because his new owner had jibbed at the high premium. He wasn't finally paid for, because of a complicated currency transfer. I had had to guarantee the money to the vendor when I didn't actually have it, and if I didn't get that two-year-old back fast and unscratched, the financial hot waters would close over my head. The foreign buyer was a ruthless man who would stop his check if the horse was damaged, and my own insurers wouldn't pay up for anything less than death, and reluctantly at that.

Sweater, jeans, boots went on at high speed and I ran downstairs fumbling to do up the buckles of the strap that anchored my shoulder. In the sitting room Crispin still snored. I shook him, calling his name. No response. The stupor persisted.

I stopped in the office to telephone the local police.

"If anyone reports a horse in their back garden, it's mine."

"Very good," said a voice. "Saves time to know."

Out in the yard there was no sound. The two-year-old had been already on the road when I woke, because it was metal on tarmac I'd heard, not the soft familiar scrunch on weedy gravel.

No sound on the road. It lay empty in the moonlight for as far as I could see.

He could be peacefully grazing the verge a few yards beyond my sight.

He could be halfway to the express line of the electric railway or on the dual carriageway to Brighton or on the main runway at the airport.

He could be crashing down rabbit holes in the local scrubby woodland.

I sweated in the cold night air. Seventy thousand bloody pounds I didn't have and couldn't raise.

Looking for a loose horse at night by car had high built-in failure factors. One couldn't hear his movements and, with his dark coat, one could hit him as soon as see him. One could startle him into panic, into crashing through a fence, tearing himself on barbed wire, skidding to his knees, damaging beyond repair the slender bones and tendons of his legs.

I hurried back through the yard, picked up a bridle and a halter from the tack room, and ran on out to the nearest paddock. There somewhere, in the dim dappled light, was the pensioned-off steeplechaser I used as a hack. Dozing on his feet and dreaming of long past Gold Cups.

Climbing the rails, I whistled to him in a trill through my teeth, the sound he responded to when he felt like it.

"Come on, boy," I called. "Come here, you bugger, for God's sweet sake." Come. Just come. But the field looked empty.

I whistled again, despairing.

He ambled over with all the urgency of a museum dinosaur. Sniffed at my fingers. Resignedly allowed me to put on his bridle. Even stood moderately still when I led him to the gate and used it as a mounting block. Jogging on his bare back, I trotted him through the yard, and at the gate let him choose his own direction.

Left lay the main roads, and right the woods. He chose the right, but as I urged him on I wondered if he had gone that way because I subconsciously wanted it. Horses, highly telepathic, needed little steering.

If the two-year-old was in the woods, he wasn't under the wheels of a twenty-ton lorry. If he was in the woods, he could be calmly eating leaves from the branches and not sticking his feet down rabbit holes. . . .

After half a mile, where the narrow road began to wind upward and the tangle of beech and bramble and evergreen grew thicker, I reined in my chaser, stood him still, and listened.

Nothing. Only the faint sound of moving air, hardly as much as a rustle. My mount waited, uninterested and unexcited. He would have known if the two-year-old had been near. He was telling me indirectly that he wasn't.

I went back, trotting him fast on the softer verge. Past the stable gate, where he wanted to turn in. Down the road to the village and across the moonlit green.

I tried to comfort myself with the thought that horses didn't usually go far when they got loose from their stable. Only as far as the nearest succulent grass. They wandered and stopped, wandered and stopped, and only if something frightened them would they decamp at a gallop. The trouble was they were so easily frightened.

There was grass enough on the village green, but no two-year-old. I stopped again on the far side, listening.

Nothing.

Worried and dry-mouthed, I went on toward the junction with the main road, where the village swept abruptly out into the three-lane double highway of the A-23.

How could I, I thought, how could I have been so stupid as not to bolt the stable door? I couldn't remember not doing it, but then I couldn't remember doing it, either. It was one of those routine actions one did automatically. I couldn't imagine not flicking the bolt when I left the box. I'd been doing it all my working life. I was not insured against my own negligence. How could I possibly—how could I ever—have been stupid enough not to bolt that door?

Even after midnight there was too much traffic on the Brighton road. Definitely not a place for horses.

I reined in again, and almost immediately my chaser lifted his head, pricked his ears, and whinnied. He twisted to the right, toward the oncoming headlights, and whinnied again. Somewhere out of sight he could hear or sense another horse, and not for the first time I envied that extra-human perception.

Hurrying, I set off southward along the green edge, hoping against hope that it was the right horse ahead and not a lay-by full of gypsy ponies.

In the distance there was suddenly a horrific screech of

tires, some wildly scything headlights, a sickening bang, and a crash of breaking glass.

My mount let out a whinny that was more a shriek. His rider felt sick.

Oh, God, I thought. Oh, dear God.

I slowed to a walk and found I was trembling. There were shouts ahead and cars pulling up, and I rubbed my hand over my face and wished I didn't have to face the next bit. Not the next hour, the next day, or the next year.

Then, unbelievably, a shape detached itself from the jumble of light and dark ahead. A shape moving very fast, straight toward me, and *clattering*.

Hoofs drummed on the hard surface with the abandon of hysteria. The two-year-old raced past at a forty-mile-an-hour full-stretched gallop, going as if the Triple Crown depended on it.

Swamped with relief that at least he was still undamaged, and blotting out fears for the car that had crashed, I swung my chaser round and set off in pursuit.

It was an unequal contest: an aging jumper against a hot-blooded sprinter. But my anxiety was spur enough for my mount. He was infected by it and aroused, and achieved a pace that was madness on that sort of surface.

The two-year-old, sensing us behind him, could have taken up the challenge and raced harder, but in fact he seemed to be reassured, not galvanized by the approach of another horse, and although he showed no sign of stopping he allowed me gradually to move alongside.

I came up on his outside, with him on my left. He had worn no head-collar in the stable, and although I had brought a halter it would have taken a circus stunt man to put it on at

35

such a gallop, let alone an unfit ex-jockey with three fused vertebrae and a shoulder that came apart with one good tug.

We were nearly back to the fork in the village. Straight ahead lay a major roundabout with crossing traffic, and the thought of causing a second accident was too appalling. Whatever the risk to the two-year-old, he had simply got to be directed into the village.

I squeezed my chaser to the left until my leg was brushing the younger horse's straining side, and I kicked my toe gently into his ribs. I did it three or four times to give him the message, and when we came to the fork, I kicked him most insistently and pulled my own mount quite sharply onto him, leaning to the left.

The two-year-old veered into the fork without losing his balance and as positively as if he had been ridden.

He fled ahead again into the village, no doubt because once we were off the main road I had instinctively slowed down. One couldn't take the narrow bends flat out.

The two-year-old discovered it the hard way. He skidded round the corner to the green, fought to keep his feet under him, struck sparks from his scrabbling shoes, tripped over the six-inch-high edge of the turf, and fell sprawling in a flurry of legs. Dismounting and grabbing the chaser's reins, I ran toward the prostrate heap. My knees felt wobbly. He couldn't, I prayed, have torn a tendon here on the soft green grass, with so much agonizing danger all behind him.

He couldn't.

He hadn't. He was winded. He lay for a while with his sides heaving, and then he stood up.

I had put the halter on him while he was down, and now led him and the chaser, one in each hand, along the lane to the yard. Both of them steamed with sweat and blew down their nostrils, and the hack, having been bridled, dripped foamy saliva from his mouth; but neither of them walked lame.

The moonlight was calming, quiet and cool. In the yard I hitched the chaser to a railing and led the two-year-old back to his box, and realized there for the first time that he was no longer wearing his rug. Somewhere on his escapade he had rid himself of it. I fetched another and buckled it on. By rights, I should have walked him round for another half-hour to cool him down, but I hadn't time, I went out, shut his door, and slammed home the bolt, and simply could not understand how I could have left it undone.

I backed the car out of the garage and drove through the village and down the main road. There was a fair crowd now at the scene of the crash, and people waving torches to direct the traffic. When I pulled onto the grass and stopped, one of the self-elected traffic directors told me to drive on, there were enough onlookers already. I told him I lived nearby and perhaps could help, and left him to move the next fellow along.

Across in the northbound lane also, the traffic was on the move, as the wreckage was all on the near side. With something like dread, I crossed over and joined the group at the heart of things. Car headlights threw them into sharp relief, bright on one side, dark on the other. All men, all on their feet. And one girl.

It was her car that was most smashed. One side of it seemed to have hit the metal post of the advance signpost to the village, and the backside of it had been rammed by a dark green Rover, which stood askew across the roadway, spilling

37

water from its dented radiator and frosty fragments from its windscreen.

The owner of the Rover was stamping about in loquacious fury, shouting about women drivers and that it was not his fault.

The girl stood looking at the remains of an orange M.G.B. GT that had buried itself nose-first into the ditch. She wore a long dress of a soft floaty material, white with a delicate black pattern and silver threads glittering in the lights. She had silver shoes and silver-blond hair, which hung straight to her shoulders, and she was bleeding.

At first I was surprised that she was standing there alone, that the masculine onlookers were not wrapping her in rugs, binding up her wounds, and generally behaving protectively, but when I spoke to her I saw why. She was in icy command of herself, as cool and silver as the moonlight. Despite the oozing cut on her forehead and the smears she had made trying to wipe it, despite the much heavier stain on her right arm and the scarlet splashes down the front of the pretty dress, she somehow repelled help. And she was not as young as she looked at first sight.

"She cut right across me," the Rover driver was shouting. "Swerved right across me! I didn't have a chance. She went to sleep. That's what she did. And now she gives us all this crap about a horse. I ask you. A horse! Swerved to avoid a horse. She went to sleep. She dreamed the horse. The silly *bitch*."

Shock took people like that sometimes and, to be fair, he had had a bad fright.

I said to the girl, "There was a horse."

She looked at me without eagerness.

"Of course there was," she said.

"Yes . . . he got loose from my stable and strayed up here onto the road."

I was immediately the focus of a hedge of accusing eyes and also the new target for the Rover driver's ire. He had really been quite restrained with the girl. He knew a lot of words one seldom heard even on a racecourse.

In a gap in the tirade, the girl spoke. She had one hand pressed against her abdomen and a strained look on her face.

"I need to go to the bathroom," she said distinctly.

"I'll take you to my house," I said. "It's not far."

The Rover driver was against it. She should stay until the police arrived, which would be at any second, he said. But some of the men showed that they understood what such an occasion could do to the viscera and silently parted to let her go with me across to my car.

"If the police want her," I said, "tell them she's at Jonah Dereham's house. First turn left, through the village, a house and stable yard out on the far side, on the right."

They nodded. When I looked back, I could see most of them returning to their own cars and driving away, and only one or two staying to support the Rover man.

She said nothing on the short journey. There was sweat on her face as well as blood. I drew up outside the kitchen and led her inside without delay.

"The cloakroom is there," I said, showing her the door.

She nodded and went inside. White walls, bright unshaded light bulb, rubber boots, waterproofs, two framed racing photographs, and an ancient shotgun. I left her to this uncozy décor and went outside again to where my chaser still patiently stood hitched to the railing.

I patted him and told him he was a great fellow. Fetched him a couple of apples from the tack room and led him back

to his paddock. He hadn't galloped so fast or felt such excitement since the day they cheered him home up the hill at
Cheltenham. He snorted with what was easy to read as pride
when I released him and trotted away on springy ankles like
a yearling.

She was coming out of the cloakroom when I returned.
She had washed the streaked blood off her face and was
dabbing the still-unclotted cut on her forehead with a towel.
I invited her with a gesture back to the kitchen, and she came
with the same marked and unusual composure.

"What you can give me now," she said, "is a large
drink."

"Er . . . How about some hot strong tea?"

She stared. "No. Brandy."

"I haven't any."

She gestured impatiently. "Whiskey, then. Gin. Anything
will do."

"I'm afraid that I haven't anything at all," I said apolo-
getically.

"Do you mean," she said in disbelief, "that you have no
alcohol of any sort in this house?"

"I'm afraid not."

"Oh, my God," she said blankly. She sat down suddenly
on the kitchen chair as if her knees had given way.

I said, "Tea is, honestly, better when you're injured. I'll
make you some."

I went over to the kettle and picked it up to fill it.

"You bloody fool," she said. Her voice was a mixture of
scorn, anger, and, surprisingly, despair.

"But . . ."

"But nothing," she said. "You let your stupid horse out

and it nearly kills me, and now you can't even save me with a bloody drink.''

"Save you?'' I echoed.

She gave me a cutting glance. Same mix: scorn, anger, despair. She explained the despair.

"Look . . . I've been to a party. I was driving myself home. Now, thanks to you and your stupid horse, there's been an accident and even though it wasn't my fault the police will be along with their little breath tests.''

I looked at her.

"I'm not drunk,'' she said unnecessarily. "Nowhere near it. But I'd be over the eighty milligrams. Even eighty-one is enough. And I can't afford to lose my driving license.''

My horse had got her into the mess. I supposed I should do my best to get her out.

"All right,'' I said. "I'll fix it.''

"Wake a neighbor,'' she said. "But do it quick, or the police will be here.''

I shook my head. I went out to the dustbin and retrieved the empty Scotch bottle.

"No time for neighbors.'' I said. "And it would look too deliberate.'' I fetched a glass and gave it to her. Then I held the empty bottle under the tap, splashed in a thimbleful of water, swilled the water around, and finally dripped it into the glass.

"Do you think,'' she said ominously, "that this is going to fool anybody?''

"Don't see why not.''

I put the empty bottle on the kitchen table and returned to the kettle. "And we'd better get your cuts seen to.''

She blotted her forehead again and looked indifferently at

the crimson state of her right forearm. "I suppose so," she said.

While the kettle boiled, I telephoned my own doctor and explained the situation.

"Take her to the casualty department at the hospital," he said. "That's what they're there for."

"She's pretty," I said. "And you'd make a better job of it."

"Dammit, Jonah, it's half past one," he said, but he agreed to come.

The tea was made and brewing by the time the police arrived with their little breath tests. They accepted mugs with sugar and milk, and sniffed sourly into the whiskey bottle and the glass in the girl's hand. Didn't she know she shouldn't have a drink before she had blown into the Breathalyzer? She shook her head tiredly and indicated that she hadn't given it a thought.

Tests within fifteen minutes of alcohol intake were not acceptable as evidence. They filled in the time by taking down her view of the facts.

"Name, Miss?"

"Sophie Randolph."

"Married?"

"No."

"Age?"

"Thirty-two." No feminine hesitation. Just a fact.

"Address?"

"Primrose Court, Scilly Isles Drive, Esher, Surrey."

"Occupation?"

"Air-traffic controller."

The policeman's pen remained stationary in the air for five seconds before he wrote it down. I looked at the girl; at

Sophie Randolph, unmarried, thirty-two, air-traffic controller, a woman accustomed to working on equal terms among males, and I remembered her instinctive reaction to the men at the scene of the crash: even in a crisis she repelled protective cosseting because in everyday life she could not afford it.

She gave them a straightforward statement. She had been to dinner with friends near Brighton. She left at twelve-fifteen. At about twelve-fifty she was driving in good visibility at forty-five miles an hour, listening to all-night radio. A horse suddenly emerged into the road from the central area of bushes. She braked hard but had no chance to stop. She steered sharply to the left to avoid the horse. She had passed the Rover a mile or so back and did not realize he was still so close behind her. The Rover struck the back of her car, slewing it round. Her car then bounced off a signpost at the side of the road, and slid to a stop in the ditch. She had been shaken. She had been wearing a seat belt. She had been slightly cut by broken glass.

One of the policemen asked what she had had to drink during the evening. In the same calm factual voice, she itemized sherry before dinner, wine with.

Eventually they got her to blow into the bag. She did so without anxiety.

The policeman who took the bag from her gave the crystals a sharp scrutiny and raised his eyebrows.

"Well, Miss," he said. "Unofficially I can tell you that if you hadn't drunk that whiskey you'd have been on the right side. It isn't much over, even now."

"I'm not really surprised," she said, and that at least was true.

"You'd be amazed the number of people who try to drink before we test them."

"Do they really?" She sounded tired, and as if evasive tactics had never come into her orbit. The police packed up their notes and their bottle kit, gave me a lecture about letting animals get loose, and in their own good time went away.

Sophie Randolph gave me the beginnings of a smile.

"Thanks," she said.

4

£

She slept in my bed and I slept in Crispin's, and Crispin slept on, unknowing, on the sofa.

She had been stitched up neatly by the doctor but had been more concerned that he should take care of her dress. She had insisted that he unpick the seam of her sleeve rather than rip the material to get to her wound, and I had smiled at the meticulous way he had snipped through the tiny threads to please her.

"My arm will mend itself," she explained. "But the dress won't, and it was expensive."

The cut, once revealed, had been jagged and deep, with fragments of glass embedded. She watched with interest while he anesthetized it locally and worked on the repairs,

45

and by the end I was wondering just what it would take to smash up such practiced self-command.

The morning found her pale and shaky but still basically unruffled. I had been going to tell her to stay in bed, but when I came in at eight-thirty after feeding and mucking out the lodgers she was already down in the kitchen. Sitting at the table, wearing my dressing gown and slippers, smoking a cigarette and reading the newspaper. There were dark smudges round her eyes and most of the thirty-two years were showing in her skin. I thought that very probably her bandaged arm was hurting.

She looked up calmly when I came in.

"Hullo," I said. "Like some coffee?"

"Very much."

I made it in the filter pot. "I was going to bring it to you upstairs," I said.

"I didn't sleep too well."

"Not madly surprising."

"I heard you out in the yard. Saw you from the window, and thought I might as well come down."

"How about some toast?" I asked.

She said yes to the toast and yes also to three strips of crispy bacon to go with it. While I cooked, she looked round the workmanlike kitchen and finally asked the hovering question. "Are you married?"

"Divorced."

"Some years ago, I would guess."

I grinned. "Quite right." Married, repented, divorced, and in no hurry to make another mistake.

"Can you lend me any clothes I won't look ridiculous in?"

"Oh . . . a jersey. Jeans. Would that do?"

"Lovely with silver shoes," she said.

I sat down beside her to drink my coffee. She had a face more pleasant than positively beautiful, a matter of coloring and expression more than bone structure. Her eyebrows and eyelashes were brownish blond, eyes hazel, mouth softly pink without lipstick.

Her composure, I began to understand, was not aggressive. It was just that she gave no one any chance to patronize or diminish her because she was female. Understandable if some men didn't like it. But her colleagues, I thought, must find it restful.

"I'm very sorry," I said. "About my horse."

"So you damn well ought to be." But there was none of the rancor she would have been entitled to.

"What can I do to make amends?"

"Are you offering a chauffeur service?"

"By all means," I said.

She munched the toast and bacon. "Well . . . I'll need to see about getting my car towed away. What's left of it. Then I'd be grateful if you could drive me to Gatwick Airport."

"Do you work there, then?" I asked, surprised.

"No. At Heathrow. But I can hire a car at Gatwick. Special discount—goes with the job."

She was using her right hand to cut the toast with, and I saw her wince.

"Do you have to work today?" I asked.

"Nothing wrong with my voice," she said. "But probably not. I'm on stand-by from four this afternoon for twelve hours. That means I just have to be home in my flat, ready to take over, at an hour's notice in case anyone is ill or doesn't turn up."

47

"And what are the chances?"

"Of working? Not high. Most stand-bys are just a bore."

She drank her coffee left-handed.

"And you?" she asked. "What do you do?"

"I'm a bloodstock agent."

She wrinkled her forehead. "I have an aunt who says all bloodstock agents are crooks."

I smiled. "The big firms wouldn't thank her for that."

"Do you work for a firm?"

I shook my head. "On my own."

She finished the toast and forked a packet of cigarettes out of my dressing-gown pocket.

"At least you smoke," she said, flicking my lighter. "I found these in your bedroom. I hope you don't mind."

"Take what you like," I said.

She looked at me levelly and with a glint of amusement.

"I'll give you something instead. That man in the Rover, do you remember him?"

"Who could fail to!"

"He was doing about forty until I tried to pass him. When I was level with him, he speeded up."

"One of those."

She nodded. "One of those. So I put my foot down and passed him and he didn't like it. He kept weaving around close behind me and flashing his headlights and generally behaving like an idiot. If he hadn't been distracting me, I might have seen your horse a fraction sooner. The crash was just as much his fault as your horse's."

"Well," I said. "Thank you, too."

We smiled at each other, and all the possibilities suddenly rose up like question marks, there in the kitchen over the crumbs of toast.

Into this subtle moment Crispin barged with the sensitivity of a tank. The kitchen door crashed open and in he came, crumpled, unshaven, ill, and swearing.

"Where the bloody hell have you hidden the whiskey?"

Sophie looked at him with predictable calm. Crispin didn't seem to notice she was there.

"Jonah, you vicious sod, I'll cut your bloody throat if you don't give it back at bloody once." It was his tragedy that he was more than half serious.

"You finished it last night," I said. "The empty bottle's in the dustbin."

"I did no such bloody thing. If you've poured it down the drain, I'll bloody strangle you."

"You poured it down your throat," I said. "And you'd better have some coffee."

"Stuff your effing coffee." He strode furiously round the kitchen, wrenching open cupboards and peering inside. "Where is it?" he said. "Where have you put it, you stinking little stableboy?"

He picked up a bag of sugar and threw it on the floor. The paper burst and the crystals scattered in a frosty swathe. He pulled several tins out to look behind them, dropping them instead of putting them back.

"Jonah, I'll kill you," he said.

I heated him some coffee and put the mug on the table. A packet of rice and another of cornflakes joined the mess on the floor.

He gave up the search with a furious slam of a cupboard door, sat down at the table, and stretched for his coffee. His hand was shaking as if he were ninety.

He seemed to see Sophie for the first time. His gaze started at her waist and slowly traveled up to her face.

"Who the bloody hell are you?"

"Sophie Randolph," she said politely.

He squinted at her. "Jonah's bloody popsy."

He swung round to me, a movement that upset his semi-circular canals and brought on an obvious wave of nausea. I hoped urgently he was not going to vomit, as he had on other vile occasions in the past.

"You lecherous bastard," he said. "All you had to do was ask me to go out. I'd have gone out. You didn't have to get me drunk."

The easy tears began to roll down his cheeks. And after the self-pity, the promises, I thought. Always the same pattern.

"You got yourself drunk," I said.

"You shouldn't have given me the Scotch," he said. "It was your bloody fault."

"You know damn well I never gave you any Scotch."

"You just put it here on the table and left it here for me to find. If that's not giving it to me, then what is?"

"You'd convince yourself it grew on a tree in the garden. You went out and bought it."

"I tell you I didn't," he said indignantly. "I just found it on the table."

He managed to get the mug to his mouth without spilling the contents.

I considered him. If by some extraordinary chance he was telling the truth, someone wished him very ill. But as far as I knew, he had no active enemies, just bored acquaintances who tended to cross the road at his approach and disappear into convenient doorways. On balance, I thought it more likely he had bought the bottle somewhere and was trying to shift the blame. The days when I could effortlessly believe what he said were ten years back.

"As God's my judge, Jonah, it was here on the table." A couple more tears oozed out. "You never believe a bloody word I say."

He drank half the coffee.

"I'd never buy whiskey," he said. "Sour bloody stuff."

Once the craving took him, he would drink whatever he could get hold of. I'd known him to pass out on crème de menthe.

He worked on the grudge that I didn't believe him until he was back to full-scale anger. With a sudden half-coordinated swing, he hurled his mug of coffee across the room, where it shattered against the wall. Brown rivulets trickled downward to the floor.

He stood up, upsetting his chair, his head lowered aggressively.

"Give me some bloody money."

"Look . . . go to bed and sleep it off."

"You stupid sod. I need it. You and your goody-goody airs. You've no bloody idea. You don't begin to understand. You've pinched my whiskey. Just give me some bloody money and go stuff yourself."

Sophie Randolph cleared her throat.

Crispin swung violently around to her to forestall any adverse suggestion she might make, and that time the sudden movement took his nausea out of control. At least he had enough self-respect left not to sick up in her face; he bolted for the back door and we could hear his troubles out in the yard, which was quite bad enough.

"He's my brother," I said.

"Yes."

She seemed to need no further explanation. She looked around at the debris. "Will he clear that up?"

"No chance," I said, smiling. "I'll do it later, when he's asleep. If I do it too soon, it enrages him. . . . He would just make a worse mess."

She shook her head in disapproval.

"He isn't like this all the time," I said. "He goes weeks sometimes without a drink."

Crispin came back looking greener than ever.

"Money," he said aggressively.

I stood up, went along to the office, and returned with five pounds. Crispin snatched it out of my hands.

"The pub isn't open yet," I observed.

"Bugger you." Crispin's gaze swung round to include Sophie. "Bugger you both."

He lurched out of the door, and through the window we watched him walk a slightly pompous path to the gate, trying to behave like a country gent and forgetting that he still wore yesterday's clothes and yesterday's beard.

"Why did you give him the money?"

"To save him stealing it."

"But—" She stopped doubtfully.

I explained. "When the craving's on him, he'll do literally anything to get alcohol. It's kinder to let him have it with some shred of dignity. He'll be drunk all today and tonight but maybe by tomorrow it will be over."

"But the pub . . ."

"They'll let him in," I said. "They understand. They'll sell him a bottle and send him home again when he shows signs of passing out."

Although to my mind she would have been better off in bed, Sophie insisted that she should be out seeing to her car.

She compromised finally to the extent of letting me ring the local garage, where I was known, and arranging the salvage. Then, dressed in jeans and sweater two sizes too big, she spent most of the morning sitting in the squashy leather armchair in the office, listening to me doing business on the telephone.

Kerry Sanders was pleased about River God and didn't quibble about the price.

"That's more like it," she said. "I never did go for that goddam name Hearse Puller."

"Well . . . I can have him fetched from Devon any time, so where and when would you like him delivered?"

"I'm visiting with the family this weekend." Even now, I noticed, she avoided using their names. "I'll be going down there for lunch and I'd like the horse van to arrive at around four-thirty."

"Certainly," I said. "What address?"

"Don't you have it?"

I said I could find it, no doubt.

She came across with the information reluctantly, as if imparting a secret. A village in Gloucestershire, as open as the day.

"O.K. Four-thirty, on the dot," I said.

"Will you be there yourself?"

"No. I don't usually."

"Oh." She sounded disappointed. "Well . . . could you make it?"

"You wouldn't need me."

"I'd sure like it," she said, her voice hovering uncertainly between cajolery and demand, and I realized that for all her assurance she was still unsure about this gift.

"You mean, to perform introductions?" I said.

"Well, I guess so."

Nicol Brevett, this is River God. River God, meet Nicol Brevett. Howdy partner, shake a hoof.

"All right," I said. "I'll arrive with the horse."

"Thanks." Again the mixture in her voice. Partly she definitely thought I ought to jump to it when asked, and partly she was genuinely relieved I had agreed. I thought she was crazy to marry into a family that made her nervous, and I wondered why they had that effect on her.

"Have you heard any more about those two men?" she asked.

"No." Apart from a sore spot when I brushed my hair, I had forgotten them. Too much seemed to have happened since.

"I'd like you to find out why they took that horse."

"I'd like to know, sure," I said. "But as to finding out . . . If you care enough, how about hiring the Radnor Halley Agency? They'd do it."

"Private detectives?"

"Specialists in racing," I said.

"Yes. Well. But . . . I don't know. . . ."

It came back every time to the way she reacted to the Brevetts.

"I'll do my best," I said, and she was pleased, but I had no confidence at all.

I spoke next to a transport firm in Devon, arranging to have them pick up River God early the following morning, and meet me at three o'clock beyond Stroud. What was the ultimate destination, they asked, and with sudden caution I didn't give it. Ten miles beyond our rendezvous, I said, and I would show them the way. I put the receiver down feeling slightly foolish, but the loss of Hearse Puller had been no joke.

I telephoned to the Devon farmer and asked him to send a man with River God to look after him, and also to produce him well-groomed, with his feet and shoes in good condition. The farmer said he hadn't the time to be bothered, and I said that if the horse looked too rough he'd get him straight back. He grunted, groused, agreed, and hung up.

"You sounded very tough on him," Sophie said, with a smile.

"Horses straight from small farms sometimes look as if they've been pulling a plow."

She lit a cigarette, the bandaged arm moving stiffly.

"I've got some codeine," I said.

She twisted her mouth. "Then I'd like some."

I fetched the pain-killers and a glass of water.

"Are you everyone's nurse?" she said.

"Mostly my own."

While I had been telephoning, she had taken note of the racing photographs on the walls.

"These are of you, aren't they?" she asked.

"Most of them."

"I've heard of you," she said. "I don't go racing myself, but my aunt has a stud farm, and I suppose I see your name in newspapers and on television."

"Not any more. It's nearly three years since I stopped."

"Do you regret it?"

"Stopping?" I shrugged. "Everyone has to, sometime." Especially when on the receiving end of six months in a spinal brace and severe warnings from gents in white coats.

She asked if I would drive her along to where she had crashed, so that she could see the place in daylight.

"Sure," I said. "And I want to look for the rug my horse got rid of on his travels, though it's bound to be torn. Pity he lost it, really, as it's a light fawn. Much easier to see in the dark than his own bay coat."

She stubbed out her cigarette, but before we could move the telephone rang.

"Hi, Jonah," said a cheerful American voice. "How did the sale go?"

"Which one?" I asked.

"Well . . . I guess the one for Kerry. You know. Kerry Sanders."

"Oh, sure," I said. "Only I've bought two for her. Didn't she tell you?"

"Uh-uh. Only that you were off to Ascot for some nag with a God-awful name."

Pauli Teksa. I pictured him at the other end of the line, a short, solidly built man in his early forties, bursting with physical and mental energy and unashamedly out to make money. I had met him only a few times and thought his most outstanding quality was the speed with which he reached decisions. After a session with him, one felt as if one had been carried along irresistibly by a strong tide, and it was only afterward that one wondered if any of his instant assessments ever turned out to be wrong.

He was over in England for the Newmarket Yearling Sales, a bloodstock agent on a large scale in the States keeping tabs on the worldwide scene.

We had had a drink together in a group of others at Newmarket the previous week, and it was because of that and other equally casual meetings that he had, I supposed, given my name to Kerry Sanders.

I told him what had become of Hearse Puller. Out of

the corner of my eye, I could see Sophie listening with
her mouth open in incredulity. Pauli Teksa's astonish-
ment was tempered by greater cynicism about the world
we both moved in, but even he was outraged at the use
of force.

"Pressure," he said vigorously. "Even unfair pressure.
Sure. But *violence* . . ."

"I'm surprised she didn't tell you."

"I've been out of town since Tuesday. Just got back from
Ireland. Guess she couldn't reach me."

"Anyway," I said, "no great harm done. She made a
profit on Hearse Puller and I bought her another horse instead."

"Yeah, but you sure ought to raise a hell of a ruckus over
what went on back there at Ascot."

"I'll leave it to Mrs. Sanders."

"It sure makes me feel bad that it was I who got you into
this mess."

"Never mind," I said.

"But I'm glad you managed to do a deal for her in the
end." He paused, his voice heavy with meaning.

I smiled wryly at the telephone. "You're saying you want
a cut of the commission?"

"Jonah, fella"—his voice sounded hurt—"did I ask?"

"I learn," I said. "I learn."

"Two percent," he said. "A gesture. Nothing more. Two
percent, Jonah. O.K.?"

"O.K.," I said, sighing. The 2 percent, which sounded
so little, was in fact two-fifths of my fee. I should have
charged Kerry Sanders more than 5 percent, I thought. Silly
me. Except that 5 percent was fair.

It was no good refusing Pauli. The remaining 3 percent

was better than nothing, even with a bang on the head thrown in, and there was good will involved. Pauli on my side was a good future prospect. Pauli against, a lousy one.

By the time I put the receiver down, Sophie had shut her mouth and regained her calm. She raised her eyebrows.

"Hey-ho for a quiet life in the country."

"Quiet is internal," I said.

Up on the main road the orange M.G. dangled like a crumpled toy at the rear of the breakdown truck. Sophie watched with regret as it was towed away, and picked up a bent silver hubcap that fell off in the first few feet.

"I liked that car," she said.

The Rover had already gone. All that remained after distance swallowed the breakdown truck were some black brake marks on the road and a pathetic heap of swept-up glass.

Sophie threw the hubcap into the ditch, shrugged off her regrets, and said we would now look for my rug.

We found it not very far away, across on the far side of the road, a damp haphazard heap half hidden by bushes. I picked it up expecting a complete ruin, as horses mostly rid themselves of their rugs by standing on one side and becoming so frightened by the unexpected restraint that they tear the cloth apart in a frenzy to get free. Horses standing quietly in stables almost never shed their rugs, but horses loose among bushes could do it easily.

"What's the matter?" she said.

I looked up. "There's nothing wrong with it."

"Well, good."

"Yes," I said doubtfully. Because I didn't see how any

horse could get out of his rug by undoing the three fastening
buckles—one across the chest, the others under the stomach—
and on this rug, which was totally undamaged, the buckles
were quite definitely undone.

5

£

Sophie was adamant about returning home, the steel in her character showing little spikes when I tried to persuade her to give my number to the people who might call her out on standby. She unbent to the extent of grilled chicken for lunch in the still-untidy kitchen, and at Gatwick Airport she even allowed me to pay the deposit for her hired car, though this was entirely because she had set out to the dinner party without checkbook or identification and felt less than impressive in my clothes. I said I liked pale blue socks with silver sandals. She said I was a bloody fool. I wished very much that she wasn't going.

Crispin's return from the pub coincided with mine from Gatwick. He was maudlin, bleary-eyed, expansive, waving his arms around in large gestures, and clutching a full bottle of gin. According to him, he didn't know how I put up with him, I was the salt of the earth, the salt of the effing earth, he didn't care who knew it.

"Sure," I said.

He belched. I wondered if one struck a match, whether gin fumes would ignite like gas.

He focused on the remains of chicken and said he wanted some.

"You won't eat it," I said.

"I will." He squinted at me. "You'll cook for a bloody popsy but not for your own brother."

I put another piece in the griller. It smelled good, looked good, and he didn't eat it. He sat at the table, picked it up in his fingers, and took a couple of small bites before pushing the plate away.

"It's tough," he said.

He lit a cigar. It took six matches, a lot of squinting, and a variety of oaths.

We'd been through so many cures. Six weeks in a private nursing home drying out, with a psychiatrist listening daily to his woes, had resulted in precisely one month's sobriety. Then, having been scooped by the police from a Park Lane gutter, he woke in a public ward and didn't like it. I told him I wasn't riding races just to keep him in trick cyclists. He said I didn't care about him. The whole hopeless circus had been going on for years.

Sophie telephoned at nine o'clock that evening. Her voice sounded so immediately familiar that it was incredible to think I had known her for less than twenty-four hours.

". . . just to thank you for everything . . ."

"For crashing your car?"

"You know what I mean," she said.

"How's the arm?"

"Oh, much better. Look . . . I don't have a lot of time. I have to go to work, after all. Rather a nuisance but it can't be helped."

"Say you don't feel up to it."

She paused. "No. It wouldn't really be true. I slept for hours when I got home and honestly I feel fine now."

I didn't argue. I already knew it was impossible to persuade her against her will.

She said, "How are your knight-in-shining-armor instincts?"

"Rusty."

"I could provide brasso."

I smiled. "What do you want done?"

"Yes. Mm. Well, when it comes to the point, I don't know that I've got any right to ask."

"Will you marry me?" I said.

"*What* did you say?"

"Er . . ." I said. "Never mind. What was it you wanted done?"

"Yes," she said.

"Yes what?"

"Yes, I will. Marry you."

I stared across the office, seeing nothing. I hadn't meant to ask her. Or had I? Anyway, not so soon. I swallowed. Cleared my throat.

"Then . . . you've a right to ask anything."

"Good," she said crisply. "Button your ears back."

"They're buttoned."

"My aunt—the one who has the stud farm—"

"Yes," I said.

"I've been talking to her on the telephone. She's in a grade-one tizzy."

"What about?"

"To be honest, I don't exactly understand. But she lives near Cirencester and I know you are going over that way tomorrow with Mrs. Sanders's horse—and—well, I suppose I sort of vaguely offered your help. Anyway, if you've got time to call on her, she'd be grateful."

"All right," I said. "What's her name?"

"Mrs. Antonia Huntercombe. Paley Stud. Her village is Paley, too. Near Cirencester."

"Right." I wrote it down. "Are you working tomorrow evening?"

"No. Saturday morning."

"Then . . . I could come to your place—on my way home—to tell you how I got on with her."

"Yes." Her voice was tentative, almost embarrassed. "I live—"

"I know where you live," I said. "Somewhere at the end of the five-furlong straight of Sandown Racecourse."

She laughed. "If I lean out, I can see the stands from the bathroom window."

"I'll be there."

"I've got to go now or I'll be late." She paused, then she said doubtfully, "Did you mean it?"

"Yes," I said. "I think so. Did you?"

"No," she said. "It's silly."

Friday morning saw the long-delayed departure of the seventy-thousand-pound two-year-old, who seemed to have suffered no harm from his nocturnal junket. I knew, as I thankfully dispatched him with his two slightly less valuable fellows, that I had been luckier than I deserved, and I still sweated at the thought of that headlong gallop down the main road.

Crispin, that Friday morning, lay in the customary coma on his bed. I rang the doctor, who said he would look in on his rounds.

"How's the girl I stitched?" he asked.

"Gone home. Gone to work."

"A lot of starch in that one."

"Yes."

I thought about her every ten minutes or so. A cool girl I had kissed once, on the cheek in the afternoon, standing beside a hired car in Gatwick Airport. She had done nothing in return but smile. One couldn't call it love. Recognition, perhaps.

Midmorning I set off for Gloucestershire, and without much trouble found the aunt's stud farm at Paley. As a business breeding venture, it had all the first-sight marks of imminent skids: weeds in the gravel, an unmended fence, tiles off the stable roof, and paint too old to keep out the rain.

The house itself was a pleasant Cotswold stone affair with too much creeper on the walls. I knocked on the front door, which was open, and was told by a rich voice to come in. Dogs greeted me in the hall—a whippet, a Labrador, two bassets, and a dachshund, all displaying curiosity tempered by good manners. I let them sniff and lick, and they'd know me next time, I thought.

"Come in, come in," called the voice.

I went farther, to the door of a long sitting room where

much-used antique furniture stood on elderly Persian rugs. Padded and pelmetted curtains and silk lampshades and Staffordshire china dogs all spoke of enough money somewhere in the past, but the holes in the worn flowery chintz sofa covers were truer of the present.

Antonia Huntercombe sat in an armchair fondling yet another dog. A Yorkshire terrier, a walking hearthrug. She was a woman of about sixty, with strong facial bones and an air of first-class stoicism in the face of titanic submersion.

"Are you Jonah Dereham?"

"Mrs. Huntercombe?"

She nodded. "Come in and sit down."

At closer quarters the voice was fruity in the lower notes and punctiliously articulated. She did not seem overfriendly, considering that I was supposed to be there to offer help.

"Excuse me not getting up," she said. "Little Dougal here is not very well, and I don't want to disturb him."

She stroked the hearthrug soothingly. One couldn't see which end of it was which.

"Sophie asked me to call," I said.

"Can't see what good you can do," she said forbiddingly. "And besides, you're one of *them*."

"One of who?"

"Bloodstock agents."

"Oh," I said. Several shades of light began to dawn.

She nodded grimly. "I told Sophie it was no good asking you for help, but she insisted that I should at least tell you my complaints. She's a very forceful girl, Sophie."

"She is indeed."

Antonia Huntercombe looked at me sharply. "She seems

65

to think well of you. She telephoned to find out how I was, but she talked mostly of you."

"Did she?"

She nodded. "Sophie needs a man. But not a crook."

I thought privately that few young women needed a man less than Sophie but quarreled only with the second half of the pronouncement.

"I'm not a crook."

"Humph."

I said, "I looked you up in the books before I came. You've got one good stallion, Barroboy, but he's getting old now, and one young one, Bunjie, who might be better if he were keener on his job. You have eight broodmares, the best being Winedark, who came third in the Oaks. She was bred last year to a top sire, Winterfriend, and you sent the resulting filly as a yearling to Newmarket Sales last week. She fetched only eighteen hundred guineas because of a heart murmur, which means that you lost a lot of money on her, as the stud fee was five thousand in the first place and then there is all her keep and care and overheads. . . ."

"It was a lie," she said fiercely.

"What was?"

"That the filly had a heart murmur. She didn't. Her heart is as sound as a bell."

"But I was there at the sales," I said. "I remember hearing that the Winterfriend filly would never race and might be doubtful even as a broodmare. That's why no one bid for her."

"That's why, right enough." Her voice was bitter. "But it wasn't true."

"You'd better tell me who spread such a rumor," I said. "Who and why."

"Who is easy. All you crooked sharks calling yourself bloodstock agents. Bloodsucking agents, more like. And as for *why*—need you ask? Because I won't give you kickbacks."

She was referring to the practice that had grown up among some agents of going to a breeder before a sale and saying, in effect, "I'll bid your horse up to a good price if you give me a share of what you get." Far more intimidating was the follow-up: "And if you don't agree to what I suggest I'll make sure no one bids for your horse, and if you sell it at all it will be at a loss." Dozens of small breeders were coughing up the kickbacks just to keep themselves in business, and Mrs. Antonia Huntercombe's difficulties were what happened if they didn't.

I knew all about it. I knew that the big reputable firms never asked for kickbacks at all, and that individual agents varied from nil to nearly extortionate.

"I was offered eight thousand for the filly," Mrs. Huntercombe said bitterly. "I was to give back half of anything she made over that price." She glared at me. "I refused to agree. Why should I? She cost eight thousand to produce. They wanted half of any profit I made. And for doing what? Nothing at all except bidding in a sale ring. No work, no worry, no thought and care. It's downright wicked to come and demand half of my profit."

"Who was it?"

"I'm not going to tell you. You're one of them, and I don't trust you."

"So you sent her to the sales to take her chance."

"She should have made at least ten thousand. At least." She glared at me. "Don't you agree?"

"Twelve or fourteen, I would have thought."

"Of course she should."

"Didn't you put a reserve on her?" I asked.

"Reserves are a racket in themselves," she said furiously. "But no, I didn't. There was no reason why she shouldn't make her price. Her breeding, her looks . . . you couldn't fault her."

"And you didn't go with her to Newmarket?"

"It's so far. And there's too much to do here. I sent a groom with her. I couldn't believe . . . I simply couldn't believe it when she went for eighteen hundred. I didn't hear that story about a heart murmur until two days afterward when the man who bought her rang up to ask for the vet's report."

I thought about the general lack of prosperity about the place.

"You needed her to make a good profit?" I suggested.

"Of course I did. She was the best foal I've had for years."

"But not the first request for a kickback?"

"The worst," she said. "I've told them all—I always tell them. . . . They've no right to what they do nothing to earn, but this time it was *wicked*."

I agreed with her. I said, "And for some time your yearlings have not been fetching good prices?"

"For two years," she said fiercely. "You're all in it. You know I won't give kickbacks so you won't bid for my horses."

She was wrong about us all being in it. I had bought several bargains at various sales when half my rivals had turned their backs. Bargains for me and my clients, disasters for the people who'd bred them. And it was always the small breeder, the honest or naïve breeder who lost, because the big firms could look after themselves and others were crooks, too, and had some scandalous tricks of their own.

The kickback system probably stemmed from the Irish "luck penny": if you bought a horse from an Irishman, he gave you back a penny of your money for luck. A penny! What a laugh.

There was no harm in a breeder giving an agent a thank-you present for getting him a good price for his horse. The harm came when the agent demanded it first. The crime came when he demanded it with threats and carried them out when he was refused.

Rumors rocketed round sale rings with the speed of light. I had heard the Winterfriend filly had a heart murmur ten minutes before she was sold, and I had believed it like everyone else.

I had often been told that the kickback lark was on the increase. Some breeders made the best of it and some positively welcomed it, because it more or less guaranteed a good price for their horses. Only the Mrs. Huntercombes who wouldn't play ball were coming to grief.

"Well?" she said belligerently. "Sophie said to ask your advice. So what is it?"

I was too much of a realist for Aunt Antonia. I knew she wouldn't like what I would say, but I said it all the same.

"You've three choices. The first is to pay the kickbacks. You'd be better off in the end."

"I won't." She narrowed her eyes in anger. "That's exactly what I would have expected from one of you."

"The second," I said, "is to sell your stud, raise a mortgage on the house, and live on an annuity."

The anger grew. "And just how do I get a fair price for my stallions and mares? And as for a mortgage—I already have one." From the way she said it, I guessed it was the largest she could get.

"Third," I said, "you could go to the sales every time when you sell a horse. Put a sensible reserve on it and get a friend to help with starting the bidding. Take a vet with you bristling with certificates. Tell the agents from the big firms, and as many other people as you can reach, that whatever they may hear to the contrary your horse is in good health, and offer to repay instantly if it is found to be not."

She stared at me. "I haven't the strength. It would be exhausting."

"You sell only six or seven a year."

"I am too old. I have high blood pressure and my ankles swell up."

It was the first really human thing she'd said. I smiled at her. She did not smile back.

"It's the best I can do," I said, standing up.

"Don't shut the front door when you go out," she said. "Or I'll have to get up to open it for the dogs."

It was barely five miles from Paley to the place beyond Stroud where I had arranged to meet the horse box bringing River God from Devon. I had expected to reach the rendezvous first, but from some distance away I could see a blue box already parked in the designated place.

I had chosen one of those useful half-moons carved by road-straightening programs where the loop of old country road remained as a leafy lay-by. There was one other car there, an old green Zodiac station wagon, which hadn't been cleaned for weeks. I passed it and the horse box, and stopped in front, getting out to go back to talk to the driver.

Talking to the driver had to be postponed, as he was

otherwise engaged. I found him standing with his back to that side of the box which faced away from the gaze of passing motorists on the main road. He was standing with his back to the box because he could retreat no farther. Before him, adopting classic threatening poses, were two men.

I knew them well enough. I had met them at Ascot.

Frizzy Hair and his mate.

They hadn't expected to see me, either, and it gave me at least an equal chance. I picked up the nearest weapon to hand, which was a nice solid piece of branch fallen from one of the road-lining trees, and positively raced to the attack. If I'd stopped to think, I might not have done it, but fury is a great disregarder of caution.

My face must have been an accurate mirror of my feelings. Frizzy Hair for one indecisive moment looked mesmerized, horrified, paralyzed by the spectacle of a normally moderate man rushing at him murderously, and because of it he moved far too slowly. I cracked the branch down on him with a ferocity that frightened me as much as him.

He screeched and clutched at the upper reaches of his left arm, and his mate made an equally comprehensive assessment of my general intentions and bolted toward the green wagon.

Frizzy Hair followed him, flinging nothing into the battle but one parting verbal shot: "It won't help you."

I ran after him, still holding the stick. He was going like a quarter horse and the mate was already in the driving seat with the motor turning over.

Frizzy Hair gave me a sick look over his shoulder, scrambled into the passenger seat, and slammed the door.

Short of being dragged along the highway, I could see no way of stopping them, but I could and did take a quick look at the mud-coated number plate as they shot away, and before I could forget it I fished out pen and paper and wrote it down.

I went much more slowly back to the driver, who was staring at me as if I were a little green man from outer space.

"Struth," he said. "I thought you was going to kill 'em."

Hell hath no fury like the vanquished getting his own back.

I said, "What did they want?"

"Blimey . . ." He pulled out a crumpled handkerchief and wiped his face. "Didn't you even know?"

"Only in general," I said. "What in particular?"

"Eh?" He seemed dazed.

"What did they want?"

"Got a fag?"

I gave him one and lit for us both. He sucked in the smoke as if it were oxygen to the drowning.

"I s'pose you are . . . Jonah Dereham?" he said.

"Who else?"

"Yeah . . . I thought you were smaller, like."

Five feet nine inches. Eleven stone. Couldn't be more average. "A lot of jump jockeys are taller," I said.

He began to look less stirred up. He ran his tongue round his teeth and seemed to feel a fresh flow of saliva to a dry mouth.

"What did they want?" I asked for the third time.

"That one you hit—with all that fluffy sort of hair—It was him did the talking."

"What did he say?"

"Rum sort of bloke. All smiley. Came up to me cab as nice as you please asking for the loan of a spanner for 'is broken-down car.'' He stopped to look at the empty road along which the broken-down car had vanished at high speed.

"Yeah . . . Well, see, I reached back to the tool kit and asked what size. Come and look see, he said. So I jumped down from me cab. And then, see, he sort of grabbed me and shoved me back against the side of the box. And he never let off smiling. Creepy bastard. So then he says, 'Look, mate, there's someone as wants this horse more than you do.' ''

"I suppose he didn't say who?"

"Eh? No. He just says there's someone as wants him more than you do, so I says it isn't mine in the first place and he says not to make jokes . . . and him laughing his bleeding head off all the time.''

"What else did he say?"

"Nothing else. Struth, he didn't have time. Well, he did say as how I'd better let him take the horse peaceful-like if I didn't want me ribs kicked in. . . . Well, I ask you—who would?''

Who indeed? "So then what?"

"That's when you came belting into them like they'd raped your sister.''

"They didn't say just how they proposed to take the horse?''

He stared. "No. I didn't ask. I s'pose they meant to drive off with the whole bleeding lot." The idea offended him. "Bleeding bastards," he said.

"Did they offer to pay for it?"

"Struth, you don't half have some funny ideas."

I wondered what they would have done if I'd given them time. I wondered if I would have found the box driver clutching the car, plus another two hundred profit, and no River God in sight.

I sighed and stubbed out my cigarette.

"Let's look at the cargo," I said, and climbed aboard the box.

The farmer had done a smartening-up job along the lines of paint over rust. The feet had been seen to: the shoes were patently new, and the newly trimmed hoofs had been darkened with oil. The mane and tail had been brushed out, and the coat was clean. On the other hand, there was a lot too much hair everywhere, which spoke of little or no regular grooming: too much mane growing between the ears, too many whiskers around the muzzle, hairs too long on the chest, hairs sticking out everywhere instead of lying down neat and flat. The whole mess was shrouded by a tatty rug with two holes in it; and there was no attendant in sight.

"I asked the farmer to send a groom," I said.

"Yeah. He said he didn't have nobody to spare. If you ask me, he isn't fit to keep a pit pony, much less a racehorse. When I got there, you'd hardly credit it; there was this poor bleeding animal standing in the yard tied up to the outside of the stable door, and there was this big bleeding pool of water all round him on the ground. Shivering, he was. I reckon they just hosed him down to get all the muck off. The farmer said he was sweating, that was why his coat looked damp. I ask you, who did he think he was kidding? I made him give me the rug to put on the poor bleeder. He didn't want me to take it in case I didn't bring it back."

"O.K.," I said. "Let's get him out."

He was surprised. "What, out here on the road?"

"That's right," I agreed.

"But he's warm enough now. He's dried off, like, on the journey up."

"All the same," I said, and helped the box driver, who said his name was Clem, unload River God. *Deus ex machina,* I thought irrelevantly, and nothing much about this one either was divine.

I removed the rug, folded it, and returned it to the box. Then, with Clem holding the horse's farm-stained head-collar, I went along to my car, took off my jacket, and in shirt sleeves collected from the trunk my bag of gear.

"What are you going to do?" Clem asked.

"Tidy him up."

"But I had to meet you at three. . . . You were early but it's a quarter past already."

"I left time enough," I said. "We're not due until four-thirty."

"Did you reckon he'd look this rough, then?"

"Thought he might."

Once I was committed to turning up with the horse, I was also committed to defend what he looked like. I took out hand clippers, two pairs of scissors, a heavy steel comb, and some wax tapers, and set to work.

Clem held the horse's head and watched while, with comb in one hand and lighted taper in the other, I worked on the rough coat, singeing out all the too long, sticking-out hair, which in a good stable would have been removed by daily brushing. The tiny candle flame was too small to disturb the horse, who felt no fear or pain, and he looked a lot less like a throwback to a cart horse when I'd finished. Next I clipped out the mane between his ears and over his withers, then snipped off the worst of the whiskers round his muzzle, and

with a large pair of scissors finally straightened the bottom
of his tail.

"Struth," Clem said. "He looks a different horse."

I shook my head. Nothing but care, good food, and brushing could bring a shine to that coat. He looked like a poor
boy after a haircut, tidy but still poor.

Before we loaded him up again, I wound neat dark blue
bandages round his forelegs and buckled on the clean rug I'd
brought from my own yard. Eliza Doolittle off to the ball, I
thought, but it was the best I could do.

6

£

Kerry Sanders looked from Nicol to Constantine in carefully camouflaged anxiety while they inspected her gift. One of Brevett's own men was showing him off, trotting him now and then or making him stand with his legs arranged as for a photograph.

River God could move, I'd give him that. A good strong walk and a straight collected trot. Nothing to be ashamed of in that department.

Constantine was saying comfortingly, "My dear girl, I realize you got him at very short notice. I'm sure he'll make up into a very good performer one of these days. Look at those legs . . . the bone is there."

"I hope he'll win for Nicol," she said.

"Of course he will. He's a very lucky boy to be given such a generous present."

The lucky boy himself drew me aside and said abrasively, "Couldn't you have found me something better?"

I had ridden against him often enough in races, at the end of my career and the beginning of his, and he knew me as well and as little as any jockey in the changing room.

"She gave me two days . . . and its form isn't bad."

"Would you have ridden it?"

"Definitely. And if it turns out no good, I'll sell it for you later."

He sucked his teeth.

"It did quite well in a bad stable," I said. "It should improve a mile in yours."

"D'you think so?"

"Give it a try."

He smiled sourly. "And don't look a gift horse in the teeth?"

"She wanted to please you," I said.

"Huh. Buy me, more like."

"Happy birthday," I said.

He turned to watch Kerry Sanders talking to his father, the neat small feminine figure overshadowed by the large protecting paternal male. As before, the Sanders wrappings were as uncluttered as gold bricks and the slanting autumn sunlight drew fire from the diamond knuckle-dusters.

"At least she's not after his money," Nicol said. "I had her checked out. She's way ahead."

For an also-ran, Constantine was not doing so badly. Clem's horse box stood on a clear quarter acre of front drive, with Clem himself fidgeting around for a signal that he could set off home. There were buildings along two sides of the mini parade ground, a modern garage and stable block at one end set at right angles to a much older, slightly austere stone house. Not quite a mansion, but more than enough for two.

The outside surface was being cleaned, with nearly a third showing warm cream instead of forbidding gray. One could see that it would look a good deal more welcoming when it was finished, but the effect meanwhile was undignified pie-bald. One should not, I reflected, ever make the mistake of thinking one would catch its master at such public disadvantage.

Nicol strode over to the man leading River God, and the man nodded and took the horse away to the stables.

Kerry Sanders looked a fraction disappointed until Nicol rejoined her and said, "Thought I'd just try it. Can't wait, you see."

River God came back with saddle and bridle, and Nicol swung easily onto his back. He trotted him a little round the gravel and then took him through a gate into a railed field alongside and quickened the pace to a working canter. Constantine Brevett watched with heavy good humor. Kerry Sanders with hope, Clem with impatience, and I with relief. Whatever I thought of his financial methods, Ronnie North had delivered the goods.

Nicol came back, handed the reins to the stableman, and strode over and with enthusiasm kissed Kerry Sanders on the cheek.

"He's great," he said. His eyes shone. "Absolutely great."

Her face was filled with joy enough to melt the hardest case. Nicol took note of it, and as she and his father turned away to go back to the house he gave me a twisted smile and said, "See? I'm not always a bastard."

"And besides," I said, "the horse is better than he looks."

"Cynical sod. It's got a mouth like the back end of a rhino."

"A ride for a pro, I was told."

"The first nice thing you've ever said to me." He laughed. "Come on in and have a drink."

"Just a sec." I turned away to go over to Clem to give him a fiver and send him off home, and found Nicol following me to double the ante. Clem took both notes with cheerfulness, hopped up into the cab, and rolled away to the gate.

Champagne stood ready in tulip-shaped glasses in the sitting room to which Nicol led the way, the last rays of sun making the bubbles glisten like silver in liquid gold. Constantine handed us a glass each and we drank rather pompously to Nicol's health. He gave me a private irreverent grin and greatly to my surprise I began to like him.

We sat in cloud-nine armchairs and Constantine fussed over Kerry Sanders. She glowed with happiness, the peach-bloom cheeks as fresh as a child's. It was extraordinary, I thought, how clearly and quickly the mental state of a woman showed in her skin.

"You almost didn't get a horse at all," she told Nicol. "The most infuriating thing happened to the first one Jonah bought."

They listened to the saga in bewilderment, and I added to it by saying that the same two thugs had tried a repeat with River God.

Constantine took up a heavily authoritarian stance, which went well with his smooth silver hair and thick black spectacle frames, and assured Kerry that he would see they got their just deserts. As it was fairly likely I had broken Frizzy Hair's arm, I thought he had probably got his already, but I had no quarrel with any plans Constantine might have for finding out what was going on. He had the weight to lean heavily in places where I had none.

"What do you think, Jonah?" Nicol asked.

"Well . . . I can't believe either Hearse Puller or River God would themselves be the cause of so much action. They came from widely different places, so it can't be anyone close to them resenting their being sold. It seems even crazier when you think that we'll find out who bought Hearse Puller as soon as he's entered in a race. Even if he's changed hands more than once, we should be able to trace him back."

Constantine shook his head heavily and spoke from personal knowledge. "Easy enough to cover up a sale if you know how."

"Maybe someone simply wanted to stop Kerry giving me a horse," Nicol said.

"But why?" Kerry asked. "Why should they?"

No one knew. "Who did you tell about River God?" I asked her.

"After last time? You must be crazy. At least when you got another horse I had the sense not to shout it around."

"You didn't tell Lady Roscommon or your hairdresser or Pauli Teksa? None of the same people as last time?"

"I sure did not. I didn't see Madge or the hairdresser guy, and Pauli was out of town."

"Someone knows," Nicol said. "So who did you tell, Jonah?"

"No one. I didn't tell the man I bought it from who it was for, and I didn't tell the transport firm where they were taking it."

"Someone knew," Nicol said again, flatly.

"Do you have any particularly bad friends?" I asked him.

"The professional jockeys all hate my guts."

"And the amateurs?"

He grinned. "Them, too, I dare say."

Constantine said, "However jealous the other riders might be of Nicol's success, I cannot see any single one of them going around buying up or stealing horses simply to prevent Nicol riding winners."

"They'd have a job," Nicol said.

Constantine's voice was resonant and deep, and filled the room to overflowing. Nicol had the same basic equipment but not the obvious appreciation of his own power, so that in him the voice was quieter, more natural, not an announcement of status.

"What about Wilton Young?" he said.

Constantine was ready to believe anything of Wilton Young. Constantine saw only one threat to his bid to dominate British racing, and that was a bullet-headed Yorkshireman with no social graces, a huge mail-order business, and the luck of the devil with horses. Wilton Young trampled all over people's finer feelings without noticing them, and judged a man solely on his ability to make brass. He and Constantine were notably alike in ruthlessness, and it was no doubt immaterial to their flattened victims that one steamroller was smoothly oiled while the other was roughly clanking.

"Of course," Constantine said, his face filling with anger. "Wilton Young."

"The two men didn't have Yorkshire accents," I said.

"What's that got to do with it?" Constantine demanded.

"Wilton Young makes a point of having Yorkshiremen working for him. He looks down on everyone else."

"Arrogant little pip-squeak," Constantine said.

"I can't honestly see him taking such trouble to stop Mrs. Sanders giving Nicol a horse for his birthday."

"Can't you?" Constantine looked down his nose as if he could believe half a dozen more improbable things before breakfast. "He'd do anything he could think of to irritate me, however petty."

"But how could he have known I was buying the horse for Nicol?"

He took barely three seconds to come up with an answer. "He saw you at the sales with Kerry, and he has seen her at the races with me."

"He wasn't at the sales," I said.

He shrugged impatiently. "All you mean is that you didn't see him."

I doubted that it was possible to be in so small a place as Ascot Sales paddock and not know whether Wilton Young was there or not. He had a voice as loud as Constantine's and a good deal more piercing, and he was not a man who liked to be overlooked.

"Anyway," Nicol said, "I'll bet his bloodstock agent was there. That carrot-headed little Yorkshireman who buys his horses."

I nodded. "So was your own chap, Vic Vincent."

Constantine had nothing but praise for Vic Vincent.

"He's bought me some great yearlings this time. Two he bought at Newmarket last week. Classic colts, both of them. Wilton Young will have nothing to touch them."

He went on at some length about the dozen or so young-sters that, according to him, were about to sweep the two-year-old board, patting himself on the back for having bought them. Vic Vincent was a great judge of a yearling. Vic Vincent was a great fellow altogether.

Vic Vincent was a great fellow to his clients, and that was about where it ended. I listened to Constantine singing his praises and drank my champagne and wondered if Vic Vincent thought me enough of a threat to his Brevett monopoly to whip away any horse I bought for the family. On balance, I doubted it. Vic Vincent looked on me as Wilton Young looked on non-Yorkshiremen: not worth bothering about.

I finished the champagne and found Kerry Sanders watching me. For signs of alcoholism, I supposed. I smiled at her and she smiled a little primly back.

"Kerry, my dear, you couldn't do better, another time, than to consult Vic Vincent."

"Yes, Constantine," she said.

From Gloucester to Esher I thought about Frizzy Hair a little and Sophie Randolph a lot. She opened her door with the composure all in place and greeted me with a duplicate of the Gatwick kiss, cheek-to-cheek, a deal too chaste.

"You found me, then," she said.

"How long have you lived here?"

"Just over a year."

"So you weren't here when I used to race next door."

"No," she said. "Come in."

She looked different. She was wearing another long dress, not white and black and silver this time, but a glowing mixture of greens and blues. The cut on her forehead had crusted over and her system had recovered from the state of shock. Her hair looked a warmer gold, her eyes a deeper brown, and only the inner self-reliance hadn't changed a jot.

"How's your arm?" I asked.

"Much better. It itches."

"Already? You heal fast."

She shut the door behind me. The small lobby was an offshoot of the sitting room that opened straight ahead, warm, colorful, and full of charming things.

"It's pretty," I said, and meant it.

"Don't sound so surprised."

"It's just . . . I thought perhaps your room might be more bare. A lot of smooth empty surfaces, and space."

"I may be smooth but I'm not empty."

"I grovel," I said.

"Quite right."

There were no airplanes on her walls, but she wore a little gold one on a chain round her neck. Her fingers strayed to it over and over again during the evening, an unconscious gesture from which she seemed to gain confidence and strength.

A bottle of white wine and two glasses stood ready on a small silver tray.

She gestured toward them noncommittally and said, "Would you like some? Or don't you ever?"

"When Crispin is drunk," I said, "I drink."

"Well, hallelujah." She seemed relieved. "In that case, take your jacket off, sit on the sofa, and tell me how you got on with my aunt."

She made no mention at all of my invitation to marry. Maybe she had decided to treat it as a joke, and yesterday's joke at that. Maybe she was right.

"Your aunt," I said, "wouldn't take my advice if I showed her the way to Heaven."

"Why not?" She handed me a glass and sat down comfortably opposite in an armchair.

I explained why not, and she was instantly angry on her aunt's behalf.

"She was swindled."

"I'm afraid so."

"Something must be done."

I sipped the wine. Light, dry, unexpectedly flowery, and definitely not supermarket plonk.

"The trouble is that the kickback system is not illegal," I said. "Far from it. To many it is a perfectly sensible business method and anyone who doesn't take advantage of it is a fool."

"But to demand half her profit—"

"The argument goes that an agent promised a large kickback will raise the auction price much higher than it might have gone, so the breeder positively benefits. Some breeders don't just put up with having to pay the kickbacks; they offer to do so. In those cases everyone is happy."

"Except the person who buys the horse," she said severely. "He comes off badly. Why do the buyers stand for it?"

"Ah," I said. "What clients don't know would sink a battleship."

She looked disapproving. "I don't like the sound of your profession." She added, in the understatement of the year, "It isn't straightforward."

"What sort of agent you are depends on how you see things," I said. "Honesty is your own view from the hill."

"That's immoral."

I shook my head. "Universal."

"You're saying that honesty in the bloodstock business is only a matter of opinion."

"And in every business, every country, every era since the world began."

"Jonah, you talk nonsense."

"How about marriage?"

"What are the kickbacks?"

"Oh, God," I said. "You learn fast."

She laughed and stood up. "I'm a lousy cook but if you stay I'll give you a delicious dinner."

I stayed. The dinner came out of frozen packs and would have pleased Lucullus: lobster in sauce on shells, and duck with almonds and honey. The freezer was the largest item in the small white kitchen. She stocked it up every six months, she said, and did practically no shopping in between.

Afterward, over coffee, I told her about Frizzy Hair turning up to take River God. It did nothing much to improve her view of my job. I told her about the flourishing feud between Constantine Brevett and Wilton Young, and also about Vic Vincent, the blue-eyed boy who could do no wrong.

"Constantine thinks the yearlings he's bought must be good because they were expensive."

"It sounds reasonable."

"It isn't."

"Why not?"

"Year after year, top prices get paid for the prize flops."

"But why?"

"Because," I said, "yearlings haven't been raced yet, and no one knows whether they will actually be any good. They make their price on their breeding." And that, too, could be rigged, though I didn't think I had better tell her.

"This Vic Vincent—he's been paying high prices for good breeding?"

"High prices for moderate breeding. Vic Vincent is cost-ing Constantine a packet. He's the biggest kickback mer-chant of the lot, and getting greedier every minute."

She looked more disgusted than horrified. "My aunt was right about you all being crooks."

"Your aunt wouldn't tell me who demanded half her prof-its . . . If you ring her again, ask her if she's ever heard of Vic Vincent, and see what she says."

"Why not right now?"

She dialed her aunt's number, and asked, and listened. Antonia Huntercombe spoke with such vehemence that I could hear her from the other side of the room, and her words were earthy Anglo-Saxon. Sophie made a face at me and nearly burst out laughing.

"All right," she said, putting down the receiver. "It was Vic Vincent. That's one of life's little mysteries cleared up. Now what about the rest?"

"Let's forget them."

"Let's absolutely not. You can't just forget two fights in three days."

"Not to mention a loose horse."

She stared. "Not the one—"

"Well," I said. "I might have believed that I hadn't shut a stable door properly for the first time in eighteen years, but not that a horse could get out of his rug by undoing the buckles."

"You said . . . he was darker without his rug."

"Yes."

"You mean someone took off his rug and shooed him out in front of my car . . . just to cause a crash?"

"To injure the horse," I said. "Or even to kill it. I'd have been in very great trouble if you hadn't reacted so quickly and missed him.''

''Because you would have been sued for your horse causing an accident?''

''No. The law is the other way round, if anything. Loose animals are no one's fault, like fallen trees. No. . . . The way the insurance on that horse was fixed, I could have lost seventy thousand pounds if he'd been damaged but not dead. And that,'' I added fervently, ''is a position I am never going to be in again.''

''Have you *got* seventy thousand pounds?''

''Along with six castles in Spain.''

''But . . .'' She wrinkled her forehead. ''Letting that horse loose means that whoever it is is attacking you personally. Not Kerry Sanders or the Brevetts . . . but you.''

''Mm.''

''But why?''

''I don't know.''

''You must have some idea.''

I shook my head. ''As far as I know, I've done no one any harm. I've thought about little else for two days but I can't think of anyone with a big enough grudge to go to all this trouble.''

''What about small grudges?''

''Dozens of them, I dare say. They flourish like weeds.''
She looked disapproving.

''You get them everywhere.'' I said mildly. ''In every working community. Schools, offices, convents, horse shows—all seething with little grudges.''

''Not in control towers.''

''Oh, yeah?''

''You're a cynic.''

"A realist. How about marriage?"

She shook her head with a smile that took the suggestion still as a joke, and her hand strayed for the twentieth time to the little gold airplane on its slender chain.

"Tell me about him," I said.

Her eyes opened wide with shock. "How did you—"

"The airplane. You wear it for someone else."

She looked down at her hand and realized how often she held it in just that position, touching the talisman.

"I . . . He's dead."

She stood up abruptly and carried the coffeepot out to the kitchen. I stood also. She came back immediately with the calm friendly face, no grief showing and no encouragement, either. She gestured to me to sit down again and we took our former places, me on the sofa, her in an adjacent armchair. There was a lot of space beside me on the sofa, but no way of getting her to sit there before she was ready.

"We lived together," she said. "For nearly four years. We never bothered to marry. It didn't seem to matter. At the beginning we never expected it to last . . . and it just grew more and more solid. I suppose we might have taken out a license in the end. . . ."

Her eyes looked back into the past.

"He was a pilot. A first officer on Jumbos, always on long trips to Australia. We were used to being apart."

Still no emotion in her voice. "He didn't die in an airplane." She paused. "Eighteen months ago yesterday, he died in a hospital in Karachi. He had a two-day rest stop there and developed an acute virus infection. . . . It didn't respond to antibiotics."

I looked at her in silence.

"I was mad to say I would marry you," she said. A smile

twitched the corners of her eyes. "It was just . . . a rather nice bit of nonsense."

"A nonsense a day is good for the digestion."

"Then you certainly will never get ulcers."

We looked at each other. A moment like that in the kitchen, but this time with no Crispin to interrupt.

"Would you consider," I said, "coming to sit on the sofa?"

"Sit on it. Not lie on it."

Her meaning was plain.

"All right."

She moved to the sofa without fuss.

"I'll say one thing for you," she said. "When you make a contract, you keep it."

"How do you know?"

"Too proud not to."

"Beast."

She laughed. She put her head on my shoulder and her mouth eventually on mine, but it was more a matter of warmth than of kindling passions. I could feel the withdrawal lying in wait only a fraction below the surface, a tenseness in the muscles warning me how easily I could go too far.

"Stop worrying," I said. "A contract's a contract, like you said."

"Is this enough for you?"

"Yes."

She relaxed a good deal. "Most men nowadays think dinner leads straight to bed."

Most men, I reflected, had exactly the right idea. I put my arm round her and shoved the most basic of urges back into its cave. I had won a lot of waiting races in my time. Patience was an old friend.

She lifted her head off my chest and rubbed her cheek.

"Something's scratching me."

I explained about the dislocating shoulder, and the strap I wore to keep it anchored in place. She traced the line of webbing across my chest and rubbed her fingers on the scratching buckle.

"How does it work?"

"A small strap round my arm is linked to the one round my chest. It stops me lifting my arm up."

"Do you wear it always?"

I nodded. "Mm."

"Even in bed?"

"Not this one. A softer one."

"Isn't it a nuisance?"

"I'm so used to it I never notice."

She looked up at my face. "Couldn't you get it fixed? Isn't there an operation?"

"I'm allergic to scalpels."

"Reasonable."

She stretched for a cigarette and I lit it, and we sat side by side talking about her job, and mine, her childhood, and mine, her tastes in books and places and people, and mine.

Exploration, not conflagration.

When the time was right, I kissed her again. And went home.

7

£

I spent most of the next week in Newmarket, staying with a trainer friend for the sales and the races.

Crispin, sober and depressed, had sworn to stay off drink in my absence and find a job, and as usual I had assured him he had the willpower to do both. Experience always proved me wrong, but to him the fiction was a prop.

Sophie had worked awkward hours all weekend and Monday, but said she would come down to my house for lunch the next Sunday, if I would like. I could bear it, I said.

The whole mob was at Newmarket. All the bloodstock agents, big and small. All the trainers with runners, all the jockeys with mounts, all the owners with hopes. All the clients with their checkbooks ready. All the breeders with their year's work at stake. All the bookies looking for mugs. All the press looking for exclusives.

I had commissions for eleven yearlings if I could find good ones at the right price, and in most cases my clients' money was already in my bank. I should have been feeling quietly pleased with the way business was expanding but found instead a compulsive tendency to look over my shoulder for Frizzy Hair.

The fact that nothing else had happened over the weekend had not persuaded me that nothing would. The attacks still seemed senseless to me, but someone somewhere must have seen a point to them, and the point was in all likelihood still there.

Crispin had sworn on everything sacred, from the Bible to his 2nd XV rugger cap, that he had found the bottle of whiskey standing ready and uncapped on the kitchen table, and had smelled it as soon as he went through the door. At the tenth vehement repetition, I believed him.

Someone knew about my shoulder. Knew about my brother. Knew I kept horses in transit in my yard. Knew I was buying a horse for Kerry Sanders to give to Nicol Brevett. Someone knew a damn sight too much.

The Newmarket sale ring would have suited Kerry Sanders: a large enclosed amphitheatre, warm, well-lit, and endowed with tip-up armchairs. At ground level round the outside, under the higher rows of seating, were small offices rented by various bloodstock agents. Each of the large firms had its own office, as did a few individuals like Vic Vincent. One had to do a good deal of business to make the expense worth it, though the convenience was enormous. I would have arrived, I thought, when I had my own little office at every major sale ring. As it was, I did my paperwork as usual in the margins of the catalogue and conducted meetings in the bar.

I turned up on the first day, Tuesday, before the first horse was sold, because often there were bargains to be had before the crowds came, and was buttonholed just inside the gate by Ronnie North.

"I got your check for River God," he said. "Now, tell me, wasn't that just what you wanted?"

"You should have seen it."

He looked pained. "I saw it race last spring."

"I shouldn't think it had been groomed since."

"You can't have everything for that money."

He was a small whippet of a man, as quick on his feet as in his deals. He never looked anyone in the face for long. His eyes were busy, as usual, looking over my shoulder to see who was arriving, who going, and what chance of the quick buck he might be missing.

"Did he like it?" he asked.

"Who?"

"Nicol Brevett."

Something in my stillness drew his attention. The wandering eyes snapped back to my face and he took rapid stock of his indiscretion.

I said, "Did you know it was for Nicol before you sold it to me?"

"No," he said, but his fractional hesitation meant "yes."

"Who told you?"

"Common knowledge," he said.

"No, it wasn't. How did you know?"

"Can't remember." He showed signs of having urgent business elsewhere and edged three steps sideways.

"You just lost a client," I said.

He stopped. "Honest, Jonah, I can't tell you. Leave it at that, there's a pal. More than my life's worth to say more, and if you want to do me a favor you'll forget I mentioned—"

"A favor for a favor," I said.

"What?"

"Start the bidding for number four."

"You want to buy it?"

"Yes," I said.

He looked at me doubtfully. No one who wanted to buy liked to show eagerness by making the first bid, but on the other hand no astute bloodstock dealer ever told another which horse he was after. I produced all the earnest naïveté I could muster and he smirked a little and agreed to bid. When he had darted off, I slowly followed, and saw him from across the paddock talking excitedly to Vic Vincent.

Together they turned the first few pages of the catalogue and read the small print. Vic Vincent shook his head. Ronnie North talked quickly, but Vic Vincent shook his head even harder.

I shrugged. All I'd proved was that Ronnie North wouldn't do me a favor without clearing it with Vic Vincent. It didn't follow that it was Vic Vincent who had told him that River God was for Nicol Brevett.

The first few horses were being led up from the stables to the collecting rings, and I leaned on the rails and took a close look at number 4. A chestnut colt grown out of proportion, with a rear end too tall for its front. Time would probably right that, but would do little to improve its narrow head. Its breeding was fairly good, its full sister had won a decent race, and it was being offered for sale by Mrs. Antonia Huntercombe of Paley Stud.

"Morning, Jonah," said a voice behind me.

I turned. Jiminy Bell, half ingratiating, half aggressive, as at Ascot. A great one for arriving unheard at one's elbow. He looked pinched with cold in the brisk wind because his overcoat was too thin for the job.

"Hullo," I said. "Care to earn a tenner?"

"You're on." No hesitation at all.

"Start the bidding on number four."

"What?" His mouth stayed open with surprise.

"Go up to two thousand."

"But you never—you never—"

"Just this once," I said.

He gulped, nodded, and presently disappeared. He was less obvious than Ronnie North, but in a remarkably short time, he, too, fetched up beside Vic Vincent, and he, too, got the emphatic shake of the head.

I sighed. Sophie's Aunt Antonia was about to make another loss. For Sophie's sake I had tried to insure her a good price, but if Vic Vincent had put the evil eye on the colt, I was going to get it for almost nothing. I thought, on the whole, that I had better not buy it. I wouldn't be able to explain it to either Sophie or her aunt.

Very much to my surprise, I found Vic himself drifting round to my side. He rested his elbows on the rails beside me, and nodded a greeting.

"Jonah."

"Vic."

We exchanged minimal smiles that were more a social convention than an expression of friendship. Yet I could have liked him, and once had, and still would have done had he not twice pinched my clients by telling them lies.

It was so easy to believe Vic Vincent. He had a large weather-beaten face, with a comfortable double chin and a full mouth that smiled easily and turned up at the corners even in repose. A lock of reddish-brown hair growing forward over his forehead gave him a boyish quality although he must have been forty, and even his twinkling blue eyes looked sincere.

The bonhomie was barely skin deep. When I had protested about my lost clients, he had laughed and told me that all was fair in love, war, and bloodstock, and if I didn't like the heat to get out of the kitchen but he would stoke up the fire as much as he liked.

He turned up his sheepskin coat collar round his ears and banged one thickly gloved hand against the other.

"Parky this morning."

"Yes."

"I heard you had a spot of bother at Ascot," he said.

"That's right."

"Constantine Brevett told me."

"I see."

"Yeah." He paused. "If Mrs. Sanders wants any more horses, you'd better let me get them."

"Did Constantine say so?"

"He did."

We watched the first horses walk round the ring. Number 4 looked reasonable from behind but scratchy in front.

"I bought a colt just like that once," Vic observed. "I thought his shoulders would develop. They never did. Always a risk when they grow unevenly."

"I suppose so," I said. Poor Antonia.

He stayed a few more seconds, but he had delivered his two messages as succinctly as if he'd said straight out, "Don't step on my toes, and don't buy that colt." He gave me the sort of reinforcing nod that the boss gives the cowed and ambled bulkily away.

The loudspeakers coughed and cleared their throats and said, "Good morning, everyone; the sale is about to begin."

I went inside. Apart from four or five earnestly suited auctioneers in their spacious rostrum, the place was deserted. Electric lights augmenting the daylight shone brightly on tiers of empty seats, and the sand on the circular track where the merchandise would walk was raked fine and flat. The auctioneers looked hopefully toward the door from the collecting ring, and Lot 1 made its apologetic appearance attended by a few worried-looking people who were apparently its vendors.

There was no bid. No one there bidding. Lot 1 made its way out through the far door and the worried people went after it.

There was no bid for Lot 2 and ditto for Lot 3. British auctioneers tended to arrange their catalogues so that the potential moneymakers came up in mid-session, and small studs like Antonia's got the cold outer edges.

Lot 4 looked better under bright lights. All horses always did, like jewelry, which was why auctioneers and jewelers spent happily on electricity.

The auctioneer dutifully started his sale while clearly expecting nothing to come of it. He stretched the price up to one thousand without one genuine bid, at which point I rather undecidedly waved my catalogue. Antonia would be livid if I got it for a thousand.

"Thank you, sir," he said, sounding surprised, and picked "Eleven hundred" expertly out of the totally empty ranks of seats facing him.

Glory be, I thought. The aunt had had the sense to slap on

a reserve. I made it twelve, the auctioneer said thirteen, and between us we limped up to his own bid of nineteen.

"You're losing him," said the auctioneer warningly.

Three or four people came in from the outside and stood near me on the edge of the track where Lot 4 plodded patiently round and round. Everyone outside could hear on the loudspeakers how the sale was going, and some had come in to see.

I wondered how high Antonia had made the reserve. Two thousand was all I would give for that colt. If she wanted more, she could have him back.

I nodded to the auctioneer. He fractionally relaxed, said smoothly, "Two thousand . . . Selling all the time now . . ." His gaze went past me to the people who had just come in. "Shall I say two thousand one?"

No one said two thousand one. He made a few more efforts to no avail, and Jonah Dereham got the colt.

I turned round. Behind me stood Vic Vincent, looking like thunder.

"Jonah," he said. "I want to talk to you."

"Sure, Vic, how about coffee?"

He brushed the suggestion aside. He took me strongly by the arm in a mock-friendly gesture and practically propelled me out the door.

"Now, look," he said.

"What's the matter?"

"I told you that colt was no good."

"I'm grateful for your interest."

He glared at me. "How much is Mrs. Huntercombe giving you?"

"It's cold out here," I said.

He looked near to fury.

"She's giving you nothing," he said.

"I haven't asked her to."

"That's the point, you stupid sod. We must all stick together. We must let the breeders know that we all stick together. Do you understand what I'm saying? We can't have you working for less than the rest of us. It's not fair on us. You'll make more money yourself, too, if we all stick together. It makes sense. Do you follow me?"

"Yes," I said. All too well.

"Mrs. Huntercombe and people like her must be made to understand that unless they reward us properly we are not interested in buying their horses."

"I follow you," I said.

"Good. So you'll go along with us in future." A positive statement, not a question.

"No," I said.

There may be quicker ways of stirring up hornets, but I doubt it. The rage flowed from him like a tangible force. He was so near to explosive physical assault that his arms jerked and his weight shifted to his toes. Only the gathering sales crowd stopped him lashing out. He flicked glances left and right, saw people watching, took an almighty and visible grip on his feelings, and put the frustrated violence into words.

"If you don't join us, we'll ruin you."

There was no mistaking the viciousness in that voice, and the threat was no idle boast. People found it easy to believe Vic Vincent. The two clients I had already lost to him had believed I cheated them, because Vic Vincent had told them so. He could stop the sale of a good filly just by saying she had a heart murmur. He could no doubt smash my growing business with a rumor just as simple and just as false. A bloodstock agent was only as secure as his clients' faith.

I could think of no adequate answer. I said, "You used not to be like this," which was true enough but got me nowhere.

"I'm telling you," he said. "You play ball or we'll get you out."

He turned on his heels and walked jerkily away, the anger spilling out of the hunched shoulders and rigid legs. Ronnie North and Jiminy Bell circled round him like anxious satellites and I could hear his voice telling them, low, vigorous, and sharp.

Within an hour most of the bloodstock agents knew of the row, and during the day I found out who my friends were. The bunch I had said I wouldn't join drew their skirts away and spoke about me among themselves while looking at me out of the corners of their eyes. The chaps in the big firms treated me exactly as usual, and even one or two with approval, as officially they frowned on exorbitant kickbacks. The uncommitted in the no man's land between were the most informative.

I had coffee and a sandwich with one of them, a man who had been in the game longer but was in much my position, more or less established and just beginning to prosper. He was distinctly worried, and cheered up not at all when I confirmed what Vic had threatened.

"They've approached me as well," he said. "They didn't say what would happen if I didn't join them. Not like with you. They just said I would be better off if I did."

"So you would."

"Yes . . . but I don't know what to do." He put down his half-finished sandwich. "They're getting so much worse."

I said I'd noticed it.

"There used to be just a few of them," he said. "When I started, only a few. But lately they're getting so powerful."

"And so greedy," I said.

"That's it," he said in eager agreement. "I don't mind a little extra on the side. Who does? It's just that they've started pushing so hard. I don't know what to do. I don't like their methods and I can't afford—" He stopped, looked depressed, and went on slowly, "I suppose I could just not bid when the word goes round. There wouldn't be much harm in that."

The make-the-best-of-it syndrome. The buttress of every tyrant in history. He took his worries away, and later I saw him smiling uneasily with Vic.

During the day, I bought one more yearling, bidding against one of the big firms and securing it for a fair price. However extensively Vic's tentacles might stretch, they had not reached every breeder in the country—or, at any rate, not yet. Neither he nor his friends showed any interest in my second purchase.

Toward the end of the day, one of my regular clients arrived with a flashy girl in one hand and a cigar in the other. Eddy Ingram, member of the well-heeled unemployed.

"Staying for the week," he said cheerfully, waving the cigar in a large gesture. "How about you joining me and Marji for dinner tomorrow night?"

"I'd like to."

"Great, great." He beamed at me, beamed at Marji. An overgrown schoolboy with a nature as generous as his inheritance. I thought him a fool and liked him a lot. "Have you found me a couple of good 'uns, then?" he asked.

"There's one tomorrow . . ."

"You buy it. Tell me after," He beamed again. "This

lad," he said to Marji, "he's bought me four horses and they've all shown a profit. Can't complain about that, can you?"

Marji smiled sweetly and said, "Yes, Eddy," which was a fair measure of her brain power.

"Don't forget, now. Dinner tomorrow." He told me where and when, and I said I would see him at the races or the sales before that, if not both.

He beamed and led Marji away to the bar, and I wished there were more like him.

In the morning I bought him a well-bred filly for eleven thousand pounds, outbidding one of Vic Vincent's cronies. As none of his bunch looked upset, I guessed that one or all of them jointly would be collecting a kickback from the breeder. Even though they hadn't bought the horse, they would collect just for raising the price.

By midmorning the crowd had swelled tremendously and almost every seat in the amphitheatre was taken. Two highly bred colts, due to come up toward noon, were bringing in the punters on their way to the races and the town's wives with their shopping baskets and the semi-drunks from the bars. None had the slightest intention of buying, but there was an irresistible fascination in seeing huge sums being spent.

I watched the two-star attractions stalk grandly round the collecting ring, and then, with the tide, I moved inside for the actual sale. No seats vacant near the door. I leaned against one of the dividing partitions and found myself next to Pauli Teksa. Short, tough, American. Wearing a wide-shouldered light blue overcoat.

"Hi," he said. "How're you doing?"

"Fine. And you?"

"Grand. . . . I hear Nicol Brevett liked his horse. Kerry called me."

"Did she tell you we nearly lost that one, too?"

"She sure did. That's some mystery you've got there."

His attention, however, was not on Kerry or me or the problem of our disappearing purchases, but on the sale in hand. Heavy scribblings and calculations surrounded the high-bred colts in his catalogue, and it looked as though one American agent at least was about to try for a slice of British bloodstock.

The double doors from the collecting ring opened and the first of the colts was led in. The crowd stirred expectantly. The auctioneers put their best man forward. Pauli Teksa cleared his throat.

I glanced at his face. Nothing relaxed about it. Strong features, hard muscles beneath the skin—a face of resolution and decision, not of kindness and compassion. He had crinkly black hair receding at the temples and smoky gray eyes that could move faster than thought.

"The first of two colts by Transporter." The auctioneer trotted through his spiel. ". . . offered for sale by the Baylight Stud. . . . Someone start me at ten thousand."

Someone started him at five. When the price rose to ten, Pauli Teksa started bidding. I owed him something, I thought, for giving me Kerry Sanders's commission, however oddly it had turned out.

"I wouldn't buy that colt if I were you," I said.

"Why not?" He raised the price another two thousand with his eyebrows.

"Because of its color."

"Nothing wrong with its color. Perfectly good chestnut." Another two thousand.

I said, "Transporter has sired about three hundred horses and that's the only chestnut. All the rest are dark bay or light brown."

"So?" Another two thousand.

"So I wouldn't bet on the paternity."

Pauli stopped bidding abruptly and turned toward me with an intent, concentrated expression.

"You sure do your homework."

I watched the chestnut colt going round the sand track while the price rose to forty thousand.

"I've seen a lot of Transporter's progeny," I said. "And they don't look like that."

The auctioneer looked over to Pauli inquiringly. "Against you, sir."

Pauli shook his head, and the bidding went on without him.

"This guy from New Zealand," he said. "When he was over Stateside, he asked me to buy him a Transporter colt at Newmarket if one came up, and ship it out to him so he could mix the bloodline with his stock."

I smiled and shook my head.

"How much do you want?" Pauli said.

"What do you mean?"

"For the information."

"Well . . . nothing."

Pauli looked at me straightly. "You're a goddam fool," he said.

"There's things besides money," I said mildly.

"No wonder these other guys are against you!"

"What have you heard?" I asked curiously.

"Why don't you go along with them?"

"I don't like what they're doing."

He gave me an old-man-of-the-world look and told me I'd get hurt if I didn't go along with the crowd. I said I would chance it. I was a triple goddam fool, he said.

The chestnut colt made fifty-six thousand pounds. The second potential star seller came into the ring looking as a Transporter should, dark bay with a slightly narrow neck and sharp pelvic bones high on the rump.

"What about this one?" Pauli demanded.

"The real McCoy."

"You slay me."

He bid for it but dropped out at his authorized limit of fifty thousand. I reflected upon how terribly easy it was to influence a sale. Pauli had believed me on two counts, first against the chestnut and then for the bay, and had acted unhesitatingly on what I'd said. Just so had others with Vic Vincent. Who could blame anyone at all for heeding off-putting advice when so much money was at risk?

At fifty-two thousand all the big firms had dropped out and the bidding had resolved itself into a straight contest between Vic Vincent and the Yorkshireman, Fynedale, who bought for Wilton Young. Constantine Brevett, I suddenly saw, had brought his smooth silver hair and dark-framed spectacles into the arena and was standing at Vic's shoulder talking urgently into his ear.

Wilton Young's man was nodding away as if he had the whole mint to call on. Constantine was looking both piqued and determined. Yearlings that cost more than sixty thousand were not a great financial proposition, even with the stud potential from Transporter, and I guessed that against anyone but Wilton Young he would have dropped out long ago.

At seventy thousand he began to scowl. At seventy-five he

shook his head angrily and stalked out of the sale ring. Fyne-dale winked at Vic Vincent.

Pauli Teksa said, "Say, that was some figure."

"Too much," I agreed.

"I guess pride comes expensive."

It did, I thought. All sorts of pride came expensive, in one way or another.

He suggested a drink and with the sale's main excitement over we joined the general exodus barward.

"Seriously, Jonah," Pauli said, glass in hand and strong features full of friendly conviction. "There's no place any more for the individualist in the game. You either have to join a big firm or else come to an agreement with the small men like yourself and act together as a body. You can't buck the system—not if you're out for profits."

"Pauli, stop trying," I said.

"I don't want to see you in big trouble, fella."

"Nothing will happen," I said, but he shook his head and said he was afraid for me, he surely was. I was too honest for my own good.

8

£

Constantine, Kerry, and Nicol were all at the track that afternoon, to see Constantine's colt start favorite for the big race. Constantine was in such a bad mood that they would have had more fun in a dentist's waiting room, and soon after they arrived Nicol detached himself from the general gloom and joined me with a grimace.

"That bloody Wilton Young . . ."

We strolled over to see the runners for the apprentice race walk round the parade ring.

"Tell your father to console himself with the thought that Wilton Young has probably poured his money down the drain."

"Do you think so?"

"How many horses earn anything like seventy-five thousand?"

"He's convinced it'll win the Arc de Triomphe."

"More likely a consolation race at Redcar."

Nicol laughed. "That'll cheer him up."

I asked him how River God was doing, and he said he was eating well and already looking better. He asked if I had found out why Frizzy Hair had wanted his horses and I said I hadn't. We spent two or three chunks of the afternoon together, cementing an unexpected friendship.

Vic Vincent took a note of it and disliked what he seemed to see as a threat to his Brevett monopoly. Even Nicol noticed the blast of ill will coming my way.

"What have you done to upset Vic?" he asked.

"Nothing."

"You must have done *something*."

I shook my head. "It's what I won't do," I said. "And don't ask what it is, because I can't tell you."

He sniffed. "Professional secret?"

"Sort of."

He gave me the flashing sideways grin. "Like when you knew I was lying my head off to keep a race on an objection, and you didn't split?"

"Well . . ."

"Yeah," he said. "I remember, even if you don't. You finished fourth. You listened to me giving my owner a right lot of codswollop and you never said a word."

"You'd won the race."

"Yeah . . . and they'd have taken it off me if you'd given me away."

"It was a long time ago."

"All of three years." He grinned. "The leopard still has the same claws."

"Spots."

"Claws." The grin came and went. "You were a ferocious bastard to ride against."

"No."

"Oh, sure. Milk and honey on the ground and a bloody nuisance as an opponent." He paused. "I'll tell you . . . I learned something from you. I learned not to go around squealing when things weren't fair. I learned to shrug off small injustices and get on with the next thing and put my energies in the future instead of rabbiting about the past. I learned not to mind too much when things went against me. And I reckon I owe you a lot for that."

"You just paid it," I said.

Later I leaned alone against the rails of the balcony on the Members' roof and looked down to where Vic Vincent was moving desultorily from group to group. Talking, smiling, taking notes, nodding, patting people on the back. He looked pleasant, knowledgeable, and useful. He looked boyish, harmless, and trustworthy. He wore a heavy tweed suit and a slightly dandified dark red shirt with a white collar and tie, and no hat on the reddish-brown hair.

I wondered why he had recently grown so aggressively rapacious. He had been successful for a long time, and as one of the top one-man bands he must have been handling about two million pounds' worth of business every year. At a flat 5 percent that meant a hundred thousand stayed with him, and even after heavy expenses and taxes he must have been well-off.

111

He worked hard. He was always there, standing in the bitter winds round the winter sales rings, totting up, evaluating, advising, buying, laying out his judgment for hire. He was working even harder now that he was going around intimidating breeders in far-flung little studs. Something had recently stoked up his appetite for money to within a millimeter of open crime.

I wondered what.

Pauli Teksa rapturized about Newmarket and compared it favorably with every American track from Saratoga to Gulf Stream Park. When pinned down by my skepticism, he said he guessed he liked Newmarket because it was so *small*. And *quaint*. And so goddam *British*. The stands at Newmarket were fairly new and comfortable; but I reflected wryly that small, quaint, and British usually meant hopelessly inadequate seating, five deep in the bars, and not enough shelter from the rain.

He liked the Heath, he said. He liked to see horses running on grass. He liked the long straight course. He liked right-handed races. He'd always liked Newmarket; it was so quaint.

"You've been here before?" I asked.

"Sure. Four years ago. Just for a look-see."

We watched an untidy little jockey squeeze home after five furlongs by a shorter margin than he ought, and on the way down from the stands we found ourselves alongside Constantine and Kerry.

She introduced the two men to each other, the big silver-haired man of property and the short wide-shouldered American. Neither took to the other on sight. They exchanged social politenesses. Constantine with more velvet than Pauli, but in less than two minutes they were nodding and moving apart.

"That guy sure thinks a lot of himself," Pauli said.

Wilton Young arrived in a helicopter a quarter of an hour before the big race. Wilton Young had his own pilot and his own Bell Ranger, which was one up on the Brevett Rolls, and he made a point of arriving everywhere as noticeably as possible. If Constantine thought a lot of himself, Wilton Young outstripped him easily.

He came bouncing through the gate from the airstrip straight across the paddock and into the parade ring, where his fourth-best three-year-old was on display for the contest.

The loud Yorkshire voice cut through the moist October air like a timber saw, the words from a distance indistinct but the over-all sound level too fierce to be missed.

Constantine stood at the other end of the parade ring towering protectively over the little knot of Kerry, his trainer, and his jockey, and trying to look unaware that his whole scene had just been stolen by the poison ivy from the skies.

Nicol said in my ear, "All we want now is for Wilton Young's horse to beat Father's," and inevitably it did. By two lengths. Easing up.

"He'll have apoplexy," Nicol said.

Constantine, however, had beautiful manners even in defeat and consoled his trainer in the unsaddling enclosure without appearing to notice the ill-bred glee going on six feet away, in the number 1 slot.

"It always happens," Nicol said. "The one you least want to win is the one that does."

I smiled. "The one you choose not to ride . . ."

"They make you look a bloody fool."

"Over and over."

At the end of the afternoon, I drove from the racecourse, which lay a mile out on the London road, down into the town again, taking the right-hand turn to the sale paddocks. Nicol came with me, as Constantine was returning with Kerry to his hotel to lick his wounds in private, and we went round the stables looking at the dozen or so yearlings I had noted as possibles. He said he was interested in learning how to buy his own horses, so that he wouldn't have to rely on an agent all his life.

"More like you, I'd be out of business," I said.

There was a filly by On Safari that I liked the look of, a big deep-chested brown mare with a kind eye. She had speed in her pedigree and her dam had produced three two-year-old winners already, and I thought that if she didn't fetch an astronomical amount she would do very nicely for Eddy Ingram.

She was due to come up about an hour after the evening session started, and I filled in the time by buying two moderate colts for a thousand each for a trainer in Cheshire.

With Nicol still in tow, I went outside to watch the On Safari filly walk round the collecting ring. She walked as well as she looked, and I feared that Eddy Ingram's limit of fifteen thousand might not be enough.

Jiminy Bell did his appearing act, sliding with a wiggle into the space between Nicol and me as we stood by the rail.

"Got a note for you," he said.

He thrust a folded piece of paper into my hand and vanished again even before I could offer him a drink, which was as unlikely as a gate-crasher leaving before the food.

I unfolded the paper.

"What's the matter?" Nicol said.

"Nothing."

I put the paper into my jacket pocket and tried to take the grimness out of my face. The message was written in capital letters and allowed for no mistakes:

DON'T BID FOR 182.

"Jonah . . . you're as tense as a high wire."

I looked at Nicol vaguely. He said again, "For God's sake, what's the matter?"

I loosened a few muscles and said flippantly, "If you've got to go, you've got to go."

"Go where?"

"I expect I'll find out."

"I don't understand you."

"Never mind," I said. "Let's go and see this filly sold."

We went into the big circular building and sat in the section of seats nearest the door, the section crowded as usual with breeders, agents, and an all-sorts mixture of racing people. Ronnie North was in the row behind us. He leaned forward and spoke into the space between our heads.

"The word is that the On Safari filly is likely to be sterile. Some infection or other . . . No good as a breeding prospect, they say. Such a pity."

Nicol looked startled and disappointed on my behalf. He asked Ronnie one or two questions, but Ronnie shook his head sadly and said he didn't know details, only that he'd heard it on the best authority.

"She wouldn't be worth so much in that case," Nicol said, turning back to me.

"Not if it's true."

"But . . . don't you think it is?"

"I don't know."

115

Lot 180 was being sold. There was so little time. "Got some business," I said to Nicol. "See you later."

I scudded to the telephone. The On Safari filly came from an Irish stud I'd scarcely heard of, and it took two precious minutes for the Irish service to find me the number. Could they ring it at once, I asked.

"Half an hour's delay."

"If it isn't at once, it will be too late."

"Hold on . . ."

There were clicks and distant voices and then suddenly, clearly, a very Irish voice saying, "Hello?"

I asked if the On Safari filly had ever had an infection or an assessment of fertility.

"Well, now," said the voice, deliberating slowly. "I wouldn't know about that, now. I wouldn't know anything about the horses, do you see, because I'm just here minding the children until Mr. and Mrs. O'Kearey get home on the train from Dublin. . . . They'll be home in an hour, so they will. They'll be able to answer your question in an hour."

When I got back, the filly was already being led round and the bidding, such as it was, had started. The seat beside Nicol had been taken. I stood in the chute through which the horses were led into the ring and listened to the auctioneer assuring everyone that she had a clean bill of health.

A man beside me shook his head dubiously. I glanced at him. A senior partner from one of the big firms. He stared morosely at the filly and made no move to buy her.

A couple of people in the crowd had taken the price up to six thousand five hundred, and there she stuck. The last bidder began to look intensely worried and obviously didn't want her. I guessed he was acting for the breeder and would have to buy the filly back if she didn't fetch a better price.

"Six thousand five . . . any advance on six thousand five? She's on the market. . . ." He looked round the ranks of blood-stock agents and took note of the shuttered impassive faces. "Six thousand five once, then. Six thousand five twice. . . . All done?" He raised his gavel and I lifted my hand.

"Six thousand six."

The last bidder's face relaxed in pure relief. Several heads turned in my general direction, looking to see who had bid, and the senior partner beside me stirred and said out of the corner of his mouth, "They say she's sterile."

"Thank you," I said.

No one else made a move. The auctioneer tried harder for another hit but without result, and knocked her down with a shake of the head.

"Jonah Dereham," he announced, writing it down.

A ripple like a shudder went through the small group round Vic Vincent. I didn't wait to hear what they had to say but beat it hastily down to the stables to see about transport. On the way back, an hour and a strong cup of coffee later, I came face-to-face with Eddy Ingram, who said loudly and without a smile that he had been looking for me.

"If you've bought that On Safari filly for me," he said positively, "you can forget it."

The bright lights around the collecting ring shone on a face from which most of the good nature had evaporated. The delectable Marji registered scorn.

"She's bound to be fast, with that breeding," I said.

"I've been told she's infected and sterile." He was angry about it. Not the usual beaming Eddy at all. "You're not spending my money on rubbish like that."

"I haven't bought you a dud yet, Eddy," I said. "If you don't want this filly—well, fair enough, I'll find someone

117

who does. But she's a bargain at that price and I'd have liked you to benefit.''

"But she's sterile. And you knew it before you bid for her. You weren't acting in my best interests.''

"Ah," I said. "Now, there's a nice phrase. Not acting in your best interest. Who said that?''

His eyes flickered. "I don't see . . .''

"I do,'' I said dryly.

"Anyway . . .'' He shrugged off his doubts. "Anyway, I'll take the one you bought for me this morning, but I don't want you to get me any more.''

Someone had been very quickly persuasive, but then Eddy was gullible and a fool. I wondered whether all my clients would desert with such speed.

Eddy came out with the clincher that had alienated him fastest. "You didn't think I would find out she was sterile. You thought you'd collect your five percent from me for buying her even though you knew she was probably useless.''

"How do you know she's sterile?'' I asked.

"Vic says so.''

"And is Vic going to buy your horses in the future?''

He nodded.

"Good luck to you, Eddy,'' I said.

He still hovered indecisively. "You haven't denied it.''

"I did not buy that filly just to get five percent.''

He began to look unhappy. "Vic said you'd deny it and I'd be a fool to believe you. . . .''

"Vic's a persuasive fellow,'' I said.

"But you've bought me four good ones. . . .''

"You sort it out, Eddy. Think it over and let me know.''

I walked away and left him.

* * *

118

An hour later, I again telephoned to Ireland.

"Is she *what*?"

I took my eardrum away from the receiver and winced.

"Of course she's not sterile." The Irish voice yelled out as if it were crossing the Irish Sea without benefit of wires. "She's never had a day's illness since she was foaled. Where the divil did you hear that?"

"At the sales."

"What?" Alarm joined the indignation. "How much did she make?"

I told him. I removed the receiver a good ten inches, and still had no difficulty in hearing. Vic Vincent's victims all seemed to be endowed with good lungs.

"I told a neighbor of mine to bid up to ten thousand and I'd be sure to pay him back if he had to buy her."

"His nerve broke at six thousand five," I said.

"I'll murder him." He sounded as if he meant to. "I told that Vic Vincent fellow I didn't need his help. I'd get my own bidding done thank you very much, and now look. Now look." He gurgled.

"What did Vic offer?" I asked.

"He said he'd raise the filly to ten thousand, and if it made more than that he wanted half. *Half!* I ask you. I offered him a fifth and that's a bloody liberty, even that much. He said half or nothing, so I said nothing and go to Hell."

"Will you do what he wants next time?"

"Next time!" The idea of a next and a next and a next time slowly sank in. "Well . . ." Some of the fire went out. There was a long pause, and when he finally spoke it was clear he had thought of the advantages of Vic's help and realized what refusing him might cost. "Well, now," he said. "Perhaps I will."

* * *

When next I saw Eddy Ingram, he was beaming away at Vic, and Marji likewise. All three of them in a little huddle, as thick as thieves.

I reflected uncharitably that I was in no way bound to tell Eddy there was nothing wrong with the filly. If she turned out to be the best broodmare of the century, it would serve him damn well right.

Toward the end of the evening, after Nicol had left to have dinner, my arm was grabbed by a man who said fiercely, "I want to talk to you," and such was the readiness of my flight reflexes that I nearly hit and ran before I realized that his grievance was not with me. He was, he said, the breeder of the Transporter colt that Wilton Young's agent Fynedale had bought for seventy-five thousand pounds. He nearly spat the words out, and did not look as one should if one's produce were among the top prices in the sales.

He insisted that he'd buy me a drink and that I should listen to him.

"All right," I said.

We stood in a corner of the bar drinking brandy and ginger ale while the bitterness poured out of him.

"I heard Vic Vincent's out to get you. That's why I'm telling you this. He came down to my place last week and bought my colt for thirty thousand."

"Oh, did he?" I said.

Private sales before the auctions were not supposed to take place. Every horse in the catalogue had to appear in the sale ring unless excused by a vet's certificate, because otherwise, as the auctioneers complained with some reason, the buyers and sellers would just use their catalogue as a free information and advertising medium, and not send their horses to the auction at all. The auctioneers produced the catalogue and set up the sales, and wanted their 10 percents for their trouble. At one or two sales the catalogue had not been produced until the very last minute, because of the number of private bargains that had been struck at other times before the auction.

Late catalogues made my job a lot more difficult. On the other hand, I knew that some breeders were avoiding paying the auctioneer's commission by selling privately for a good sum and then doing everything they could to keep the auction price at rock bottom. One couldn't blame the auctioneers for fighting back.

"Vic gave me a double promise," said the breeder, his lips tight with fury. "He said they wouldn't bid the price up to thirty thousand if nobody else was trying to buy."

"So that you wouldn't have to pay the full commission to the auctioneers?"

He stared. "Nothing wrong in that, is there? Business is business."

"Go on," I said.

"He said that if the price went up to fifty thousand he would give me half of everything over thirty."

He drank, nearly choking himself. I watched.

"And then—then—" He spluttered, hardly able to get the words out. "Do you know what he has the gall to say? He says our agreement only went as far as fifty thousand. Everything over that, he takes it *all*."

I admired the beauty of it in an odd sort of way.

"Was the agreement in writing?" I asked.

"Yes," he said furiously.

"Unfortunate."

"*Unfortunate!* Is that all you have to say?"

I sighed. "Why didn't you let the colt take its chance at the sale instead of selling to Vic first?"

"Because he didn't think it would make as much as thirty at auction, but he had a client who would give that much, and he said I might as well benefit."

"Have you ever dealt with Vic before?" I asked curiously.

"Not directly. No. And to be honest, I was flattered when he came to my place specially. . . . *Flattered!*"

He crashed his empty glass with a bang onto one of the small tables scattered in the bar. A man sitting at the table looked up and waved a beckoning arm.

"Join the club," he said.

I knew him slightly: a small-scale trainer from one of the northern counties who came down south occasionally to buy new horses for his owners. He knew as much about horses as any agent, and I reckoned his owners had been lucky he could buy for them himself, as it saved them having to pay an agent's commission.

He was lightly smashed, if not drunk.

"That bastard," he said. "Vic Vincent. Join the anti-Vic Vincent club."

The breeder, hardly attending, said, "What are you talking about?"

"Can you beat it?" the trainer asked of the world in general. "I've bought horses for an owner of mine for years. Damn good horses. Then what happens? He meets Vic Vincent and Vic persuades him to let him buy him a horse. So he buys it. And then what happens? Then I buy him a horse, like I've always done. And then what happens? Vic Vincent complains to my owner, saying I shouldn't buy the horses because it does him, Vic Vincent, out of the fair commission he would be getting if he bought them. Can you believe it? So I complain to my owner about him buying horses through Vic Vincent because I like to train horses I choose, not horses Vic Vincent chooses, and then what do you think happens?''

He threw his arms wide theatrically and waited for his cue.

''What happens?'' I supplied obligingly.

''Then my owner says I'm not being fair to Vic Vincent, and he takes his horses away from me and sends them to another trainer that Vic Vincent picked out for him, and now between them they're rooking my owner right and left, but he doesn't even realize, because he thinks horses must be twice as good if they cost twice as much.''

The breeder listened in silence because he was deep in his own grudges; and I listened in silence because I believed every incredible word of it. People who bought racehorses could be more easily conned than any old lady parting with her savings to a kind young man on a doorstep. People who bought racehorses were buying dreams, and would follow anyone who said he knew the way to the end of the rainbow. A few had found the crock of gold there, and the rest never gave up looking. Someone ought to start a Society for the Protection of Gullible Owners, I thought, smiling, with Constantine and Wilton Young as its first cases.

The breeder and the trainer bought large refills and sat down to compare wounds. I left them to their sorrows, went back to the ring, and bid unsuccessfully for a well-grown colt that went to Vic Vincent for nearly double my authorized limit.

The underbidder was Jiminy Bell. I saw Vic giving him a tenner afterward and patting him on the back. Some other Gullible Owner would be paying Vic. It was enough to make you laugh.

* * *

Vic was not laughing, however, in the car park.

I was fishing out my keys to unlock the car door when someone shined a torch straight at my face.

"Turn that bloody thing off," I said.

The light went out. When the dazzle cleared from my eyes, there were seven men standing round me in a ring at a distance of six feet.

I looked at them one by one. Vic Vincent and the carrot-headed Yorkshireman Fynedale, Ronnie North and Jiminy Bell. Three others I met every day at the sales.

All deadly serious.

"What have we here?" I said. "A lynch mob?"

No one thought it funny. Not even me.

9

£

Vic said, "You're going to have to be told, Jonah."

"Told what?"

There were people within shouting distance, going to their cars. I thought maybe I would shout, but not perhaps just yet.

The seven men took a small step forward almost as if moved by a signal. I stood with my back against my car and thought I was getting tired of being attacked in car parks. Have to travel more by train.

"You're going to do what we tell you, whether you like it or not."

"No." I said. "I am not."

125

They took another step and stood in a solid wall, shoulder to shoulder. If I reached out, I could touch them.

"You'll fall over yourselves in a minute," I said.

They didn't like me trying to make a joke of them. The anger Vic had throttled earlier rose up again in his face, and none of his clients would have recognized their friendly neighborhood bloodsucker. A vein in his forehead swelled and throbbed.

The Yorkshireman Fynedale put his shoulder in front of Vic's as if to hold him back.

"You're more trouble than you're worth," he told me. "And you might as well get this straight. You're not to bid when we say not. Right?"

Vic elbowed him back. Vic didn't like his lieutenant usurping the role of number 1 thug.

"If we get rough, you've asked for it," he said.

"Get," I said. "What do you call that bang on the head at Ascot? A friendly pat?"

He snapped out. "That wasn't us," and instantly regretted it. His face closed like a slammed door.

I glanced round the ring of faces. Some of them didn't know what had happened at Ascot. But Vic did. Fynedale did. Ronnie North and Jiminy Bell did. . . .

"Who was it?"

"Never you mind. You just reckon you've had a taster. And you bloody will do what you're told."

They all looked so furiously intent that I wanted to laugh, but when they suddenly wheeled away and went off to their own cars I found I didn't want to laugh after all. I stood where they'd left me and breathed in deep lungfuls of winter night. However ludicrous I might think it that some perfectly ordinary citizens should threaten to beat me up if I didn't join their strong-arm union, their collective menace had been real enough.

All I suddenly wanted was a cigarette.

There were few cars left in the park, but the one next to mine turned out to be Pauli Teksa's.

"Jonah?" he said, peering at me through the dim lighting.

"Hullo."

"You're just standing there smoking?"

"Yeah."

"Want to come to my place for a bite to eat?"

By tacit consent my dinner date with Eddy and Marji had lapsed, but my hosts for the week were not expecting me back. If I wanted to eat at all, it might as well be in company.

"Couldn't think of anything better," I said.

He was staying in a pub outside Newmarket, which put on late dinners especially for people after the sales. The cozy bar and dining room were full of familiar faces and the general conversation was predictable.

He moved his strong stocky body through the crowd with ease, and there was some quality about him that parted the crush like Moses and the Red Sea. I watched him being served at the bar at once where others had waited longer, and saw that the others acknowledged rather than resented his priority. I wondered what it must be like to be Pauli, generating such natural and unconscious power.

We ate smoked salmon and then roast pheasant, and drank Château Haut-Badon '70, which was my choice, not his, as he said Americans knew goddam all about French wines and he was no exception. He preferred bourbon, he said.

He gave me a cigar from a crocodile case with gold mountings. A Havana. He inhaled the smoke deeply, and sighed, and said the only good thing ever to come out of Cuba was its cigars and life in the States was hardly worth living now they were banned. He had stocked up in England, he said. He was going to smuggle a hundred or so through in his baggage.

"You looked a bit shook up back there in the car park," he said.

"Did I?"

"Those guys I saw standing round you when I came out of the gate. They friends of yours?"

"Business acquaintances."

He smiled sympathetically. "Ganging up on you, eh? Well, I sure did warn you."

"You sure did," I said, smiling back.

He looked at me assessingly. "They don't seem to have made it stick."

"No."

"You want to take care, fella," he said earnestly. "Remember you got bashed at Ascot."

"Tonight's lot said they didn't do that."

He was surprised. "They said?"

I nodded. "They clammed up as soon as they'd said it. It might be true in a way, because the two men who took Hearse Puller and tried to get River God aren't regulars on the racing scene. I'd never seen them before. But at a guess—tonight's crowd supplied the basic information."

"How do you mean?"

"Between them they knew everything the two strangers knew."

"What sort of things?"

His strong face was intent, receptive, helpful. I told him

about the two-year-old getting loose on the main road, and about Crispin's whiskey.

He was astounded. I said, "Of the people there tonight, Jiminy Bell knew about my dicey arm, as he'd seen the strap often enough in the changing room when we were both jockeys. Ronnie North knew I'd bought River God, because he'd sold it to me. Vic Vincent knew I kept horses in transit in my yard. Any of them could have known I have an alcoholic brother; it's no secret. All of them were at Ascot the day I bought Hearse Puller. It's quite clear they could have supplied the info if they'd wanted to. The trouble is that I simply don't see the point."

He carefully edged half an inch of ash off the end of his cigar and took his time over replying.

"I'll tell you what they might have been after," he said.

"What?"

"To soften you up."

"What?" I laughed. "You can't be serious."

He shrugged. "It's possible. They rough you up a little. Nothing you'd make too much of a fuss of. Kick you around a bit. Then they give out with the threats. . . . Join us or else."

I shook my head. "It can't be that simple."

"Why not?"

"Because I'm not that much of a threat to them. Why should they go to all that trouble?"

He leaned back in his chair, smiling gently through the Cuban smoke. "Don't you know the classic law of the invader, fella? Single out the strongest guy around and smash him. Then all the weaker crowd come to heel like lambs."

"Vic has invaded like the Mongol hordes," I agreed, "but I'm by no means the strongest guy around."

"You sell yourself short, fella."

"Don't be a nut."

He shook his head. "I back my own judgment. Make my decisions. Buy my horses. Quick. Snap." He snapped his fingers. "And I don't get things wrong."

The circus left Newmarket after the races on Saturday.

By that time relations between Vic and me were, if possible, worse. He had instructed me not to bid on five occasions; three of those yearlings I hadn't wanted anyway, and the other two I bought. The mood of the mob had hardened to the point where I was careful to keep out of lonely car parks.

By Saturday, Vic had warned Constantine that I was not a good companion for Nicol. Constantine had warned Nicol, and Nicol grinning over a sandwich, had warned me.

Wilton Young had become the owner of three more yearlings at near-record prices and Fynedale was smirking from ear to ear.

Constantine had pretended not to be mortified, and had cheered up considerably when his horse beat Wilton Young's in the Cesarewitch.

Eddy Ingram asked to have the On Safari filly, after all, as he had discovered on his own account that she was undamaged, but I had already passed her on to another client and felt regrettably unsympathetic when I told him so.

On the business side I had had quite a good week in spite of all Vic's threats, but I drove away down the A-11 to London with a deep sigh of relief.

The relief lasted until I turned down toward the village at home.

The village was in a turmoil, with all the people out of the houses and the street blocked with cars, bicycles, prams, and kids. The time was ten past eight. The cause of the upheaval was a bright glow in the night sky with leaping flames and flying sparks, and I knew at once and without hope that the place on fire was mine.

It was impossible to drive there. I left my car and went forward on foot, competing—it seemed to me—with every man, woman, and wheelchair in the parish. The nearer I got the more I had to push; it was a six-deep seething mass that was being held back by a portable barrier placed across the gateway. I squeezed round one end of it to get into the yard and was roughly told by a busy fireman to get out.

"It's my bloody house," I snapped. "I've just got home."

"Oh." He paused fractionally. "The wind's against us, I'm afraid. We're doing our best."

I looked around me and took stock.

The stables were alight and gone. Bright orange from end to end. Flames shot up high from what had been the roof, roaring and crackling like thunder and lightning shaken together in some demoniacal cocktail. The heat was incredible. Smoke swirled everywhere, stinging the eyes. It was like being on the wrong side of a giant bonfire, and I could see what he had meant by the wind. It was blowing showers of bright splintery sparks like rain into the still black bulk of the house.

Half the firemen were trying to damp down the stables. The rest, back-to-back and cramped for room, were focusing on what might still be saved. Silver jets of water swept the tiles and the back of the house and poured through my bedroom window, which was broken.

There were two fire engines, both of them through the

other side of the yard, out in the paddock. I wondered stupidly what they were doing there, and then realized they were pumping water directly from the brook, which ran along one side. Not a very big brook, I thought uneasily. The long narrow yard itself was a sea of puddles and hoses and men in black helmets doing a difficult job efficiently, part-time firemen who'd left their Saturday-night beer in the local pub and come out enthusiastically to try to save my house. It was crazy to think of their beer at a time like that, but I did.

The fireman I'd spoken to before said sympathetically that I'd had a hell of a homecoming. He said that there was never much hope for places like stables and farms once they caught fire, not if there was any hay or straw stored there. Burned like tinder, he said.

"We sent for another appliance," he said. "It ought to be here by now." He had almost to shout for me to hear.

"The road's blocked right back into the village," I said.

He looked resigned, which was not what I felt.

"Sorry about your car," he shouted.

"What car?"

He swept an arm round to the garage at the end of the stable block and pointed. The remains of Crispin's car were burning in there like a skeleton.

I caught the fireman by the arm.

"Where's my brother?" I shouted. "He's here. . . . Where is he?"

He shook his head. "The place was empty. We checked. The fire hadn't got such a hold when we came, and there was no danger inside the house then."

"He might be asleep."

"No one could have slept through this lot, mate," he

132

shouted and, looking and listening to the disaster, one could see his point.

"I'll have to make sure."

"Come back!" he yelled. "You can't go in there now. You'll suffocate."

He fielded me forcibly on my way to the kitchen door. I said we must find my brother.

He began to tell me again that he wasn't there.

"He might be dead drunk." It was no time to save Crispin's face. "Unconscious." And he might have walked down to the pub and be sitting there obliviously over his sixth double gin; but I couldn't waste time finding out.

"Oh." The fireman pulled me through the scrum of men and hoses to the nearest fire engine and thrust a breathing pack into my arms.

"Put it on," he said. "The lights will be shot to hell by now, and you can find him quicker than I can, if he's there." He gave me a helmet and gloves and we ran over to the house, with me struggling to fasten everything on.

The house was unbelievably full of smoke—dark, pungent, hot, and oily. The only light was from the flames outside, which meant that all the far rooms were filled with black fog. It stung in my eyes worse than ever and made them water. I straightened the breathing mask over them and tried to see where I was going.

"Where would he be?" yelled the fireman.

"Maybe the sitting room. This way."

We blundered down the passage and into the pitch-black room. Impossible to see. I felt all over the sofa, the armchairs, and the floor around, which was where he usually passed out.

No Crispin.

"No good."

We went upstairs. Everything was very hot indeed up there and the smoke was, if anything, denser. Patches of wood-work round the door were charred, as if they had already burned, but there were no actual flames.

I couldn't find him anywhere in his bedroom, which was dark, or in mine, which glowed vividly orange through the smoke and was as drenching as a tropical rainstorm from the water pouring through the window.

"He isn't here," shouted the fireman.

"Bathroom . . ." I said.

"Hurry. The roof's smoldering."

The bathroom door was shut but not locked. I opened it, took one step, and tripped over Crispin's feet.

The air in there was clearer. The fireman pushed past me, threw Crispin over his shoulder as if he were a child, and went out of the house faster than I could with no burden.

He laid Crispin on a patch of wet grass because there was nowhere else to put him. I pulled off the breathing mask and looked down at him anxiously.

"Is he alive?"

"Don't know. Put your mask on him."

He started at once giving Crispin artificial respiration by the method of pulling his arms backward over his head, while I clipped on the mask and checked the airflow.

Without pausing, the fireman glanced up at the staring crowd at the gate and at the rows of faces looking over the hedge for as far down the road as the flames lit them, and I could read his mind as if he'd spoken. The third appliance, an ambulance, doctor, police—no other vehicle was going to reach us until the village went home.

* * *

The roof down the half of the stables nearest us fell in with a roar and a sudden outgushing of sizzling heat. The fireman raised his eyes from his exertions on Crispin and said encouragingly, "Now if the rest of that roof falls in quickly, the house has more of a chance."

I looked up. The incendiary shower of sparks had diminished, but the house looked more than ever as if it would burst all over into flames in explosive spontaneous combustion. Despite all the firemen's efforts, the eaves at the far end were blackly burning.

Crispin showed not the slightest sign of life, but when I felt for his pulse, it was there. Faint and slow, but there.

I nodded to the fireman in relief, and he stopped the respiration. He watched Crispin's chest. There was no perceptible movement. The fireman slid his hand inside Crispin's clothes to feel his ribs. Nothing. He shook his head, and went back to pumping.

"I can do that," I said.

"Right."

I took his place and he went back to help with the fire, and the hot roaring smoky nightmare seemed to go on and on and on.

Crispin lived and they more or less saved the house.

At some point that I wasn't quite clear about, the police arrived, and soon afterward an ambulance took my still unconscious brother away to a more thorough decoking.

The first thing the firemen told the police was that it looked like arson, and the first thing the police asked me was had I started it.

"I wasn't even here."

"Have you got any money troubles?"

I looked at them incredulously. Standing there in all that shambles, with thick hot smoke still pouring off the damp and blackening embers, they were stolidly conducting inquiries.

"Is that all the help you can give?" I said, but their manner said plainly enough that they weren't there to give help.

It seemed the final unreality on that disjointed night that they should believe I had brought such destruction on myself.

By dawn, one of the fire engines had gone but the other was still there, because, the firemen told me, with old houses you never knew. Sometimes a beam would smolder for hours, then burst into flames and start the whole thing over again.

They yawned and rolled up hoses, and smoked cigarettes that they stubbed out carefully in little flat tins. Relays of tea in thermos flasks came up from the village, and a few cautious jokes grew like flowers on the ruins.

At nine I went down to the pub to borrow the telephone, and caught sight of myself in a mirror. Face streaked with black, eyes red with smoke and as weary as sin.

I told Sophie not to come, there wouldn't be any lunch. She would come anyway, she said, and I hadn't the stamina to argue.

The pub gave me a bath and breakfast. My clothes smelled horrible when I put them on again, but nothing compared to the house and yard when I got back. Wet burnt wood, wet burnt straw, stale smoke. The smell was acrid and depressing, but the departing firemen said nothing could be done; things always smelled like that after blazes.

Sophie came, and she was not wearing the gold airplane. She wrinkled her nose at the terrible mess and silently put her arm through mine and kissed me. I felt more comforted than I had since childhood.

"What's left?" she said.

"Some wet furniture and a tin of peanuts."

"Let's start with those."

We went through the house room by room. Watery ash and stale smoke everywhere. My bedroom had a jagged black corner open to the sky where the roof had burned right through, and everything in there was past tense. I supposed it was lucky I had had some of my clothes with me in New-market.

There was an empty gin bottle in Crispin's room, and another in the bathroom.

In the office the ash covered everything in a thick gritty film. The walls were darkened by smoke and streaked with water and my rows of precious, expensive, and practically irreplaceable form books and stud records would never be the same again.

"What are you going to do?" Sophie said, standing on the filthy kitchen floor and running one finger through the dust on the table.

"Emigrate," I said.

"Seriously?"

"No . . . Seriously, the pub opens in five minutes and we might as well get drunk."

10

We rolled home happily at two o'clock, and found the police there. Two of them, one a constable, one with the shoulder badges of Chief Inspector.

"Enjoying yourself, Mr. Dereham?" the Chief Inspector said sarcastically. "Celebrating on the insurance money, are you?"

It seemed, however, that this opening was more a matter of habit than threat, because they had not, after all, come to accuse, but to ask and inform.

"Chilly out here, sir," the Chief Inspector said, looking up pointedly at the dull wintry sky.

"Chilly indoors now, too," I said. "The central-heating oil tank was in the stables."

"Ah," he said. "Yes, exactly."

All the same, he chose to go indoors, so I took them into the office and fetched a duster for the chairs. The duster merely smeared the dirt, I had to fetch others for them to spread out and sit on.

"Tell us about your enemies, Mr. Dereham," said the Chief Inspector.

"What enemies?"

"Exactly, sir. What enemies do you have?"

"I didn't know I had any who would set fire to my stable."

"You may not have known it before, sir, but you know it now."

I nodded.

"Give us a name, sir."

"I don't think I can. But it isn't the first thing that's happened." I told them about Hearse Puller, and about my loose two-year-old, and the Chief Inspector asked immediately why I hadn't reported these things to the police.

"I did report the Ascot incident," I said, thanking Kerry's indignation. "And, as for the horse, some of your men came here after the accident, but I didn't think then that the horse had deliberately been let loose. I thought I'd just been careless."

As they had thought the same thing, they could hardly quarrel with that. The Chief Inspector also knew perfectly well that they wouldn't have called out the reserves if I'd turned up with the unbuckled rug.

"Well, sir," he said. "It seems you were lucky this time. We have a witness. A fourteen-year-old boy who'd been up in the woods at the end of your lane. He was going home. He says he saw what he saw from the lane, but I reckon he'd come here to help himself to what was lying around loose.

He says he knew you were away in Newmarket. Anyway, he said he saw a man go into the storeroom in the stable block, and he heard him making metallic noises in there, and thought it odd that whoever it was had not switched the lights on. He seems to know his way round your stables pretty well. He saw the man strike a match and bend down. Then the man came out of the stable and hurried away along the lane to the village. The boy didn't try to intercept him, but went to the storeroom and switched on the light.''

The Chief Inspector paused, with a fine sense of theatre. His riveted audience waited impatiently for him to get on with it.

''He took one look and retreated without delay. He says the pipe from the oil storage tank at the back of the stove was broken and the oil was coming out onto the floor. Standing in the pool of oil was a cardboard box, and on that there was a large firework. A golden shower, he says. He observed that the touch paper was red and smoking. He did not advance into the storeroom, he says, because in his opinion anyone who had done so would have needed his brains examined— that is, if his brains hadn't been burning with the rest of him.''

Sophie laughed at his verbatim bit of reporting. The Chief Inspector permitted himself the smallest of smiles.

''Anyway, sir, it seems he then made best speed down the village to tell his mum to call the Fire Brigade, which, once he had convinced her, she did. When the firemen arrived here, the oil tank had exploded and the stables, being built internally largely of wood, were hopelessly alight. The firemen say that if they had arrived much later they could not have saved the house.''

He smiled lopsidedly. "They usually ruin what they only just save."

"The house is fine," I said.

"Good. Now, what young Kenneth saw is not evidence that you didn't set the whole thing up yourself. People often arrange to have fires start while they themselves have an unbreakable alibi."

Sophie started to protest. The Chief Inspector gave her an amused glanced, and she stopped abruptly.

"All right, Miss. This time it's different. This time we know a bit more. Young Kenneth gave us a description of the man he saw."

"But it was dark," I said.

"Something about the man was very distinctive. Apart from that, we found the car he came in. After everyone had gone home last night, there were two cars left in the village street. One was yours. One was a Zodiac station wagon, and the man Kenneth had seen here was reported as having been observed trying to start it, failing to do so, kicking its wheels in disgust, and walking towards the main road, presumably to thumb a lift. Upon examining the station wagon, we found two things. One was that the starter motor had jammed and that was why it would not start. The other was that the number plates did not coincide with the number written on the license. We checked the license. The car belongs to a Mr. Leonard Williamson, who says a young fellow took it away from him. He was asked if he knew the young fellow's name and eventually he said he did. The young fellow was a Mr. Frederick Smith. We went to the home of Mr. Frederick Smith and invited him to come down here and help with our inquiries."

"Or, in other words," I said, smiling, "Leonard Williamson shopped Fred Smith, who is now swearing blue murder in one of your cells."

The Chief Inspector said primly, "We would like you to come and see if you know him."

It was Frizzy Hair.

He looked hard, arrogant, and unrepentant. The taunting smile he gave his victims had become a taunting sneer for his captors, and the way he sprawled on a chair with his legs spread wide was a statement of defiance.

You could see at once why young Kenneth had been able to describe him. On his left arm, from biceps to knuckles, he wore a large white plaster cast.

He stared boldly at me without recognition.

"Hello, lover boy," I said.

The Chief Inspector looked at me sharply. "So you do know him."

"Yes. He attacked me at Ascot."

"I never."

"Mrs. Kerry Sanders saw you."

He blinked. Remembered. Narrowed his eyes with a snap, and gave me a look that would have done credit to a crocodile.

"You broke my bleeding elbow."

"I never," I said.

"I hear your stable burnt," he said viciously. "Pity you weren't in it."

The Chief Inspector drew me back to his office.

"He's got form as long as your arm," he said cheerfully. "Well known on his own patch, is Fred Smith."

"Someone's paying him," I said.

"Oh, yes. But we've no chance of him telling us who it

is. He's hard as nails. The Fred Smiths of this world never grass.'' He sounded as if he admired him for it. ''He'll do his time, but he'll tell us nothing.''

Sophie came with me to see Crispin, who was sick and sorry for himself in the local hospital. His skin was pallid and sweaty, he coughed with a hand pressed to his chest, and his eyes showed that the gin level had ebbed as far as maximum agony. Like an axe chopping his brain, he'd once described it.

The first thing he said when he saw us was ''Give me a bloody drink. They won't give me a bloody drink.''

I produced a small bottle of orange juice. He stared at it balefully.

''You know what I bloody mean.''

''Yes,'' I said. ''Vitamin C. Marvelous for hangovers.'' I poured the orange juice into a glass and gave it to him. A nurse watched approvingly from across the room. Crispin sniffed it crossly, tasted it, and drank the lot. He lay back against his pillows and closed the swimmy eyes.

''Bloody orange juice,'' he said.

He lay for a minute or two as if asleep but then, with his eyes still shut, said, ''I hear you saved my bloody life.''

''Not exactly.''

''Near enough. . . . Don't expect me to be grateful.''

''No.''

Another long pause. ''Come and fetch me tomorrow morning,'' he said. ''About noon, they said.''

''All right.''

''As for now, you can bugger off.''

Sophie walked away with me down the ward with her disgust escaping like steam.

"Why on earth do you put up with him?"

"He's my brother."

"You could kick him out."

"Would you?"

She didn't answer. When it came to the point, one couldn't.

I thought of him lying there in his acute self-made misery, a lonely defeated man in a private hell. He'd had girl friends once, but not any more. There was no one except me between him and the gutter, and I knew he relied on me as if I'd been a solid wall.

"Isn't there any cure?" Sophie said.

"Oh, yes. One certain cure. The only one."

"What is it?"

"Wanting to be cured."

She looked at me dubiously. "Does that make sense?"

"He would automatically be cured if his urge to be cured was stronger than his urge to drink."

"But sometimes it is," she said. "You said he sometimes doesn't drink for weeks."

I shook my head. "He always means to drink again. He just postpones it, like a child saving its sweets."

We collected my car and drove off toward the ill-smelling cinders.

"I thought it was a disease," she said.

"An addiction. Like football."

"You've been at the nonsense again."

"Under the influence of football," I said, "you can tear railway carriages apart and stampede people to death."

"More people die of alcohol," she protested.

"I expect you're right."

"You're having me on."

I grinned.

144

"I thought there was a drug that could cure it," she said.

"You mean antabuse?"

"What's that?"

"Some stuff that makes alcohol taste disgusting. Sure, it works. But you've got to want to stop drinking in the first place; otherwise you don't take it."

"Crispin won't?"

I nodded. "You're so right. Crispin won't."

"How about Alcoholics Anonymous?" she asked.

"Same thing," I said. "If you want to stop drinking, they're marvelous. If you don't, you keep away from them."

"I never thought about it like that."

"Lucky old you."

"Pig."

We went a mile or so in companionable silence.

"All the same," she said, "I've always been told it was an illness. That you couldn't help it. That one drink sets off a sort of chain reaction."

"It isn't the one drink. It's the wanting to drink. Alcoholism is in the mind."

"And in the legs."

I laughed. "O.K., it invades the body. In fact, the bodies of ultra-persistent alcoholics become so adjusted chemically to the irrigation that a sudden cutoff in the supply can cause epileptic fits."

"Not . . . in Crispin?"

"No. Not so bad. But when he says he needs a bloody drink, he needs it."

Which was why the drink I'd given him had been only half orange juice and the other half gin.

* * *

We stood in the yard for a while with the last of daylight fading over the cooling embers of the stables.

"What are you thinking?" Sophie said.

"Oh . . . That I'd like to break Fred Smith's other elbow. Also his knees, toes, ankles, and neck."

"In that order," she said, nodding.

I laughed, but the inner anger remained. This time the assault had been too much. This had gone beyond a skirmish to a major act of war. If Pauli Teksa was by any chance right and Vic or someone besides him was trying to frighten me off the scene, they were having the opposite effect. Far from persuading me to go along with Vic's schemes, they had killed the tolerance with which I had always regarded them. In my own way I could be as bloody-minded as frizzy Fred Smith. Vic was going to wish he had left me alone.

I turned away from the ruins. I would rebuild what had been lost. Soon, and better, I thought.

"Where are you planning to sleep?" Sophie asked.

I looked at her in the dusk. Smooth silver-blond hair. Calm sky-reflecting eyes. Nothing but friendly interest.

Where I was planning to sleep was going to need more welcome than that.

"Could I borrow your sofa?" I said.

A pause.

"It's not long enough," she said.

Another pause. I looked at her and waited.

A smile crept in around her eyes.

"Oh, all right. You gave me your bed. . . . I'll give you mine."

"With you in it?"

"I don't suppose you burned your bedroom just to get there?" she asked.

"I wish I could say yes."

"You look smug enough as it is," she said.

We drove sedately to Esher, she in her car, I in mine. We ate a sedate dinner out of her freezer, and watched a sedate old movie on her box.

She was also, in a way, sedate in bed. The inner composure persisted. She seemed to raise a mental eyebrow in amusement at the antics humans got up to. She was quiet, and passive.

On the other hand, she left me in no doubt that I gave her pleasure; and what I gave, I got.

It was an intense, gentle lovemaking. A matter of small movements, not gymnastics. Of exquisite lingering sensations. And done, on her part also, without reservation.

She lay afterward with her head on my shoulder.

She said, "I can't stay here till morning."

"Why not?"

"Have to be at Heathrow on duty by six o'clock."

"Fine time to say so."

I could feel her smile. "Better than ten minutes ago."

I laughed in my nose. "The off-put of the century."

She rubbed her hand lazily over my chest. "I'll think of this when I'm up in the tower."

"You'll knit the approaches."

"No." She kissed my skin. "I'm on departures. I tell them when to take off."

"When?"

"And where. But not what."

I smiled. Shut my eyes in the warm dark.

"You don't take your strap off even for lovemaking," she said, running her fingers along inside the soft crêpe bandage I slept in.

"Especially," I said. "Very high risk activity for dislocating shoulders."

"You speak from experience?"

"You might say so."

"Serve you right."

We slid slowly, contentedly, to sleep.

11

£

At Ascot Sales on Wednesday, Vic and his pals closed their ranks when they saw me coming, and moved in my direction as a body.

I met them halfway. Like something out of *High Noon*, I thought frivolously. All we lacked were the sheriff's badge and the guns.

"I warned you," Vic said.

They stared at me. I looked at them one by one. Vic was all open aggression, the rest in various shades from satisfied spite to a trace of uneasiness.

"People who play with fire get burnt," I said.

Vic said, "We didn't do it."

"Quite right. Fred Smith did. And he's not telling who paid him. But you and I know, don't we, Vic?"

He looked extraordinarily startled. "*You* know?" he exclaimed. "You couldn't." He considered it and shook his head. "You don't."

"But *you* know," I said slowly. "And if it isn't you, who is it?"

Vic gave a fair imitation of a clam.

"You just do as we tell you and nothing else will happen," he said.

"You've got your psychology all wrong," I said. "You bash me, I'll bash back."

Jiminy Bell said to Vic, "I told you so."

Vic gave him a reptilian glance. Jiminy was a great one for losing friends and not influencing people.

Ronnie North stood on one side of their battalion commander and Fynedale on the other. Neither of them looked impressed or worried about my vaguely stated intentions.

"How about a truce?" I suggested. "You leave me entirely alone, and I'll leave you."

Seven upper lips curled in unison.

"You can't do a damn thing," Vic said.

I bought four horses for various clients uninfected by Vic, and went home. Crispin, morosely sober, had spent the day watching a demolition gang shift the burnt rubble of the stables into lorries. The stale smell persisted, and the air was full of dust and fine ash, but the hard concrete foundations had been cleared and cleaned in some places and looked like the first outlines of the future.

He was sitting in the office drinking fizzy lemonade in front of a television program for children. Two days had seen rapid action by the electricity people, who had insulated all burnt-through wires and restored the current, and by the post office, who had reconnected me with the outer world. With help from the village I had cleaned up the office and the kitchen and borrowed dry beds, and even if the house was partly roofed by tarpaulin and as sodden as an Irish bog, it was still where I lived.

"About twenty people telephoned," Crispin said. "I've had a bloody awful day answering the damn thing."

"Did you take messages?"

"Couldn't be bothered. Told them to ring again this evening."

"Have you eaten anything?"

"Someone brought you an apple pie from the village," he said. "I ate that."

I sat down at the desk to make a start on the ever-present paperwork.

"Get me some lemonade?" I asked.

"Get it yourself."

I didn't, and presently, with an ostentatious sigh, he went out to the kitchen and fetched some. The thin synthetic fizz at least took away the taste of brick dust and cinders, though as usual I wished someone would invent a soft drink with a flavor of dry white wine. A great pity all soft drinks were sweet.

During the evening, apart from answering the postponed inquiries and finalizing various sales, I made three more personal calls.

One was to the breeder of the Transporter colt that Vic had bought for thirty thousand and let go to Wilton Young for seventy-five.

One was to Nicol Brevett. And one to Wilton Young himself.

As a result of these, the breeder met Nicol the next day in Gloucester, and on the Friday morning I drove them both to see the mail-order tycoon in Yorkshire.

The row between Wilton Young and his carrot-headed agent at Doncaster races that Saturday could be heard from Glasgow to The Wash. Along with everyone else, I listened avidly and with more than general satisfaction.

Wilton Young had not wanted to believe he had been made a fool of. What man would? I was wrong, he said. His agent Fynedale would never conspire with Vic Vincent to drive the price of a colt up by thousands so that he, Wilton Young, would shell out, while they, the manipulators, split the lolly between them.

I hadn't said much at the interview. I'd left it all to the breeder. The furious indignation he'd been exploding with at Newmarket had deepened into a bitter consuming resentment, and he had pounced like a starving cat on the opportunity of doing Vic a lot of no good.

Nicol himself had been astounded and angry on his father's behalf and had sat next to me all the way to Yorkshire saying, at regular intervals, that he couldn't believe it. I was sure Nicol's surprise was genuine but I privately doubted whether Constantine's would be. Nicol's father was quite subtle enough to make Wilton Young pay and pay and pay for the privilege of outbidding a Brevett. That was, of course, if his pride would allow so private a victory, and on that point I was in a fog.

Wilton Young and Fynedale stood on the grass in front of the weighing room shouting at each other as if oblivious of the fascinated audience of five thousand. Wilton Young attacked like a tough little terrier and Fynedale's temper burned as flaming bright as his hair. One or two Stewards hovered on the perimeter looking nervous about the outcome, and the jockeys on their way out to the first race went past with smiles like watermelon slices.

". . . barefaced bloody fraud!" Wilton Young was shouting, the Yorkshire accent thick and blunt. "I tell thee straight, no one makes a bloody monkey out of me and gets away with it. You don't buy no more horses for me, I tell thee straight. And I want back from you every penny you've swindled out of me these past two years."

"You've no bloody chance," scoffed Fynedale, driving nails into his own coffin with the recklessness of all hotheads. "You paid a fair price for those horses, and if you don't like it you can bloody lump it."

"A fair price to you and that damned Vic Vincent is every penny you can screw out of people who trust you. All right, I've been a right bloody fool, but that's all finished. I tell thee straight." He stabbed the air with his forefinger, emphasizing every angry word. "I'll sue you for that money, see if I don't."

"Don't bother. Thee'll not win."

"Enough mud'll stick on you to save any other mugs wasting their brass. I tell thee straight, Mister, by the time I've finished, every single person in this country is going to know they pay through the bloody nose for every horse you buy them."

"I'll bloody sue you for libel!" Fynedale yelled.

"And it'll be bloody worth it."

"I'll take you for millions!" Fynedale screamed, almost jumping up and down with fury.

"You do already."

The row hotted up in noise level and degenerated to straight abuse, and when the race began the unprintable insults rose in volume above commentary. Along with many others, I was chuckling so much I couldn't hold my race glasses still enough to watch the distant runners. Nicol, standing beside me, had tears running down his cheeks.

"Oh, my God," he said, gasping for breath. "What is a fat-arsed hyena-faced bloodsucking son of a sodding bitch?"

"A mongrel," I said.

"Oh, don't. It hurts." He pressed a hand to his heaving ribs. "It's too much."

Even after the main row was over, little eddies of it persisted all afternoon, both Wilton Young and Fynedale separately being anxious to air their grievances loudly to all who would listen. Wilton Young's forefinger stabbed the air as if he were poking holes in it and Fynedale's voice took on a defensive whine. I kept away from them for most of the time, but before the end they both came looking for me.

Wilton Young said, "Like a bloody piece of quicksilver, you are. I keep seeing you in the distance, and then when I go that way you've disappeared."

"Sorry," I said.

"You were right and I was wrong. There you are, then." He made a large gesture of magnanimity, letting me know how generous he thought himself to be making such an admission. "The little tyke was swindling me. Like you said. All legal-like, mind. I've been told this afternoon I won't have a chance of getting anything back."

"No," I said.

"Cut your losses, that's what I always say. Any line in my

mail-order business that's not pulling its weight, I scrap it. Same with my horses. Same with employees, see?''

''I see.''

''You don't approve. I can see it in your face. You're soft, lad, you'll never get anywhere.''

''Depends where you want to go,'' I said.

He stared, then laughed. ''Right, then. You go to the sales next week and buy me a horse. Any horse you think is good. Then we'll see.''

''Good for what?''

''A fair return for outlay.''

''In cash terms?''

''Naturally in cash terms. What else is there?''

If he didn't know, I couldn't tell him.

''I wasn't born in Yorkshire,'' I said.

''What the hell has that got to do with it?''

''You only employ Yorkshiremen.''

''And look where it bloody got me. No, lad, you buy me a good horse and I'll overlook you being born in the wrong place.''

Nicol drifted near, and Wilton Young gave him a stare suitable for the son of his dearest enemy, even if the two of them had the common bond of victims.

''Another thing you can do for me,'' Wilton Young said to me, stabbing the inoffensive air. ''Find me a way of taking that effing Fynedale for every penny he screwed out of me. I tell thee straight, I'll not rest till I'm satisfied.''

I hesitated, but I'd already gone a long way down the road. I said slowly, ''I do know—''

He seized on it. ''What? What do you know?''

''Well . . .'' I said. ''You remember those three horses you sent out to race in South Africa?''

"Damned waste of good money. They had useful form here, but they never did any good in Durban. The climate was all wrong. And of course they couldn't come back because of the quarantine laws."

"One died soon after it arrived in South Africa," I said. "And the other two never saw a racecourse."

He was surprised. "How the hell do you know?"

"They went by sea," I said.

"They didn't, then," he interrupted positively. "They went by air. Had a bad flight, by all accounts."

"They went by sea," I said. "I sent two horses out there, and they went on the same boat. I sent a groom with mine, and quantities of food. Your three traveled alone for three weeks with no one to look after them. They were shipped with a total of half a ton of hay—and not even good hay, at that. No oats, bran, or horse cubes. Just a starvation ration of poor hay, and no one to see that they even got that. The man I sent looked after them as best he could and gave them enough of my food to keep them alive, but when they reached Durban they were in such a poor state that they were almost not allowed into the country."

He listened in disbelief. "I sent them by air," he repeated.

"You thought you did. I read in the *Sporting Life* that they'd flown out to Durban. But when my man came back, he told me what had really happened."

"But I paid for air. . . . I paid more than four thousand quid."

"And who did you pay?"

"By God." He looked murderous. "I'll screw him to the wall, I tell thee straight."

"Get a lawyer to do it," I said. "I'll tell him which ship

it was, and give him the name and address of the groom I sent.''

"By God, I will," he said. He turned on his heel and hurried off as if going to do it there and then.

Nicol said, "When you start a fire, you do it properly."

"They shouldn't have burned my stable."

"No," he said. "That was a bad mistake."

Fynedale's anger was in a different category altogether. He caught me fiercely by the arm outside the weighing room and his face made me determined to stay in well-lit populated places.

"I'll kill you," he said.

"You could have had a truce," I said.

"Vic will kill you."

It sounded ridiculous. Fynedale might do at a pinch, but Vic wasn't the killing sort.

"Don't be silly," I said. "You two can't even light your own fires. And Fred Smith won't kill me for you; he's in clink."

"Someone else will."

"Jiminy Bell?" I suggested. "Ronnie North? You're all good at using threats but you need a Fred Smith to carry them out. And Fred Smiths don't grow on trees."

"We keep telling you," he said fiercely. "We didn't pay Fred Smith. We didn't tell him to burn your yard. We didn't."

"Who did?"

"Vic did. No . . . Vic didn't."

"Sort it out."

"Vic reported that you wouldn't play ball. He said you needed a bloody good lesson."

"Reported to who?"

"How do I know?"

"You ought to find out. Look where he's got you. Out of a cushy job with Wilton Young and into a nasty prosecution for fraud. You're a bloody fool to let someone you don't know get you into such a mess."

"*You* got me into the mess!" he yelled.

"You bash me, I bash back."

The message at last got through, and the result on him was the same as it had been on me. Aggression created counter-aggression. The way full-scale wars started. He expressed no sorrow. Made no apologies. No offer of amends. Instead he said again and with increased intention, "I'll kill you."

Nicol said, "What are you going to do next?"

"Pork pie and a bottle of Coke."

"No, you ass. I mean about Vic."

"Stoke up his kitchen fire." Nicol looked mystified. I said, "He told me once if I didn't like the heat . . ."

"To stay out of the kitchen."

"Right."

The cold dank winter afternoon seeped under my anorak and my feet were freezing. Nicol's face looked pale blue. A little kitchen heat would have done no harm.

"How?"

"Not sure yet."

It had been comparatively easy to break up the entente between Wilton Young and Fynedale, for the two hotheaded Yorkshire tempers had needed only a small detonation to set them off. Detaching Constantine from Vic might take longer. Constantine was not as bluntly honest as Wilton Young, and in his case face-saving might have priority.

"There's also someone else," I said.

"Who?"

"Don't know. Someone helping Vic. Someone who engaged Fred Smith to do the dirty work. I don't know who . . . but I won't stop until I find out."

Nicol looked at me speculatively. "If he could see the look on your face, he'd be busy covering his tracks."

The trouble was, his tracks were far too well covered already. To find him, I'd have to persuade him to make fresh ones. We went into the snack bar for the warmth as much as the food and watched the fifth race on closed-circuit television.

Nicol said, "Do you know of any other fiddles Vic and Fynedale have got up to?"

I smiled. "One or two."

"What?"

"Well . . . there's the insurance-premium fiddle."

"What's that?"

"I shouldn't be telling you."

"Things have changed. You don't owe them a scrap of loyalty any more."

I wryly agreed. "Well . . . Say you sell a horse to an overseas customer. You tell him you can arrange insurance for the journey if he sends the premiums. So he sends the premiums, and you pocket them."

"Just like that?"

"Just like that."

"But what happens if the horse dies on the way? Surely you have to pay up out of your own money?"

"You say you were very sorry you couldn't arrange the insurance in time, and you send the premiums back."

"By God."

"By the time you've finished, you should be more clued up than your father," I said with amusement.

"I should damn well hope so. Vic's been taking him for one almighty ride."

"Caveat emptor," I said.

"What does that mean?"

"Buyer beware."

"I know one buyer who'll beware for the rest of his life, and that's me."

The next week, and the Newmarket Mixed Sales, I bought a two-year-old colt named Singeling for Wilton Young.

He was there himself.

"Why that one?" he demanded. "I've looked him up. He's run in three races and never been nearer than sixth."

"He'll win next year as a three-year-old."

"How do you know?"

"Scorchmark's progeny need time to grow. It's no good being impatient if they don't win at two. He's being sold by an impatient owner and he's been trained by a two-year-old specialist. They both wanted quick results, and Singeling wasn't bred for that. Next summer he'll win."

"He didn't cost very much," he said disparagingly.

"All the better. One good prize and he'll be making you that profit."

He grunted. "All right. I said buy me a horse, and you've bought it. I won't go back on my word. But I don't think that Singeling is any bloody good."

Owing to the natural loudness of his voice, this opinion was easily overheard, and a little while later he sold Singeling himself to someone who disagreed with him.

With typical bluntness he told me about it. "He offered me a good bit more than you paid. So I took it. I didn't reckon he'd be much good, that Singeling. Now, what do you have to say to that?''

"Nothing," I said mildly. "You asked me to buy you a horse that would give you a good return in cash terms. Well . . . it has.''

He stared. He slapped his thigh. He laughed. Then a new thought struck him and he looked suddenly suspicious. "Did you find another buyer and send him to offer me a profit?''

"No," I said, and reflected that at least he seemed to be learning.

"I'll tell you something," he said grudgingly. "This chap I sold it to—when we'd shaken hands on it and it was too late for me to back out, he said—I tell thee straight—he said any horse Jonah Dereham picked as a good prospect was good enough for him.''

"Flattering," I said.

"Aye." He pursed his mouth and screwed up his eyes. "Maybe I was too hasty, getting rid of that Singeling. I reckon you'd better buy me another one, and I'll keep it, even if it's got three legs and a squint.''

"You positively ask to be cheated," I said.

"You won't cheat me."

"How do you know?"

He looked nonplused. Waved his arms about. "Everybody knows," he said.

Vic was not his confident cheerful self. He spent a great deal of his time drawing people into corners and talking to them vehemently, and in due course I learned that he was saying I was so desperate for clients I was telling outright lies about sincere men like Fynedale, and that I had a fixed obsession that he, Vic Vincent, had set fire to my stables, which was mad as well as wicked, because the police had arrested the man who had really done it. I supposed the extent to which people believed his version was a matter of habit: his devotees never doubted him, or if they did they kept it to themselves.

Vic and Pauli Teksa stood alone together on the far side of the collecting ring, with Vic's tongue working overtime. Pauli shook his head. Vic spoke faster than ever. Pauli shook his head again.

Vic looked around him as if to make sure he was not being overheard, then advanced his head to within three inches of Pauli's, his red-brown forward-growing hair almost mingling with Pauli's crinkly black.

Pauli listened for quite a while. Then he drew back and stood with his head on one side, considering, while Vic talked some more. Then slowly again he shook his head.

Vic was not pleased. The two men began to walk toward the sale building—or, rather, Pauli began to walk, and Vic, unsuccessfully trying to stop him, had either to let him go or go with him. He went, still talking, persuading, protesting.

I was standing between them and the sale building. They saw me from four paces away, and stopped. Vic looked as lividly angry as I'd ever seen him, Pauli as expressionless as a concrete block.

Vic gave Pauli a final furious look and strode away.

Pauli said, "I plan to go home tomorrow."

There were some big American sales the next week. I said, "You've been here a month, I suppose. . . ."

"Nearer five weeks."

"Has it been a successful trip?"

He smiled ruefully. "Not very."

We went together for a cup of coffee, but he seemed pre-occupied.

"I'd sure like to have bought a colt by Transporter," he said.

"There'll be another crop next year."

"Yeah . . ."

He said nothing more about me going along with the crowd, with conforming unless I got hurt. What he did say, though, with his mind clearly on his recent encounter, was "You don't want to stir up that Vic Vincent more than you can help."

I smiled.

He looked at the smile and read it right. He shook his head.

"He's an angry man, and angry men are dangerous."

"That makes two of us," I said.

He soberly consulted his stock of inner wisdom and came up with a cliché. "It's easier to start something than to stop it."

12

£

Wilton Young came to the following Doncaster Sales not to buy but to see some of his horses in training sold. Cutting his losses, he said. Weeding out all those who'd eaten more during the just-ended flat season than they'd earned. He slapped me jovially on the back and told me straight that slow horses ate as much as fast, and he, Wilton Young, was no meal ticket for flops.

"Profit, lad," he boomed. "That's what it's all about. Brass, lad. Brass."

I bought one of his castoffs, a three-year-old colt with little form and a reputation for kicking visitors out of his box. I got him cheap for a Sussex farmer who couldn't afford more.

His ex-owner said disparagingly, "What did you buy that

164

for? It's no bloody good. If that's what you buy, what the hell will you buy for me?''

I explained about the poorish farmer. ''He'll geld it and hack it about the farm. Teach it to jump. Make it a four-year-old novice hurdler by April.''

''Huh.''

Second-rate jumpers were of less account than marbles to self-made tycoons with checkbooks open for Derby prospects. I realized that whatever his fury against Fynedale he was still expecting to pay large sums for his horses. Perhaps he needed to. Perhaps he felt a reflected glory in their expense. Perhaps he wanted to prove to the world how much brass he'd made. Conspicuous consumption, no less.

Which meant that to please him best I would have to buy an obviously good horse at a shade above what I thought it worth. Given a bargain like Singeling, he had rid himself of it within an hour, and for all his twinge of regret afterward he would likely do the same again. Accordingly I picked out the pride of the sale, a two-year-old with near-classic expectations, and asked if he would like it.

''Aye,'' he said. ''If it's the best, I would.''

''It'll fetch at least twenty thousand,'' I said. ''How far do you want me to go?''

''It's your job. You do it.''

I got it for twenty-six, and he was delighted.

Fynedale was not.

From across the ring his eyes looked like stark black holes in his chalk-white face. His hair flamed like a burning sash. The hate vibrated in him so visibly that if I could have seen his aura it would have been bright red.

* * *

Constantine had brought Kerry to the Friday sales, although the chief purpose of their journey to Yorkshire was to see Nicol try out River God in Saturday's novice chase.

Constantine was saying authoritatively to whoever would listen that keeping a large string of horses in training was becoming impossibly expensive these days, and that he thought it a prudent time to retrench. Only fools, he intimated, were still ready to buy at the inflated prices of recent months.

I saw Vic Vincent go across to greet them when they came. Amicable handshakes. Smiles with teeth. A good deal of window dressing to establish that whatever some people might think of their agents, Constantine was satisfied with his.

Nicol came and leaned beside me on the rail of the collecting ring.

"I told him," he said. "I said Vic had been rooking him of thousands. Vic and Fynedale, pushing up the prices and splitting the proceeds."

"What happened?"

He looked puzzled. "Nothing. He didn't say much at all. I got the impression—I know it's silly—but I got the impression he already knew."

"He's nobody's fool," I said.

"No . . . but if he knew, why did he let Vic get away with it?"

"Ask him."

"I did. He simply didn't answer. I said I supposed he would ditch him now and he said I supposed wrong. Vic could pick horses better than any other single agent, he said, and he had no intention of cutting himself off from his advice."

We watched the merchandise walk round the collecting ring. Nothing in the current bunch looked worth the outlay.

Nicol said gloomily, "They think I'm a traitor for listening to you at all. You're absolutely *persona non grata* with my parent."

Predictable. If Constantine wasn't going to admit he'd been swindled, he wouldn't exactly fall on the neck of the person who'd publicly pointed it out.

"Is he really cutting down on his string?" I asked.

"Heaven knows. He's not noticeably short of the next quid, though some big deal or other fell through the other day, which irritated him more than somewhat." He gave me a quick sideways sardonic glance. "My new stepmama will be able to maintain us in the style to which we are accustomed."

"Why don't you turn professional?" I asked with mild reproof. "You're good enough."

I had, it seemed, touched him on a jumpy nerve. He said angrily, "Are you trying to tell me I should earn my own living?"

"Not really my business."

"Then keep your trap shut."

He shifted abruptly off the rail and walked away. I didn't watch him go. A minute later he came back.

"You sod," he said.

"I try."

"You bloody well succeed."

He hunched his shoulders inside his sheepskin coat. "Professional jockeys aren't allowed to own horses in training," he said.

"Nothing to stop them running in your father's name."

"Shut up," he said. "Just shut up."

I shut.

* * *

I came face to face with Vic by accident, he coming out of the sale building, I going in. He was moderately triumphant.

"You've got nowhere," he said.

"Because you'll soon find another stooge to replace Fynedale?"

His mouth compressed. "I'm admitting nothing."

"How wise."

He gave me a furious look and stalked away. He'd said nothing this time about me toeing the line or else. Perhaps because with Fynedale out of action there was no effective line to toe. Perhaps the "or else" campaign was temporarily in abeyance. Nothing in his manner persuaded me it was over forever.

Having Wilton Young for a client positively galvanized my business. During that one Friday, I received as many inquiries and definite commissions as in any past whole month, mostly from northern trainers with bustling would-be owners who, like Wilton Young, had made their own brass.

As one trainer for whom I'd ridden in the past put it, "They know off-all about horses but the money's burning their fingers. All they want is to be sure they're getting the best possible. That they're not being done. Get me ten good two-year-olds and I'll see you right."

Both Vic and Fynedale noticed the constant stream of new clients and the swelling of my order book: they would have to have been blind not to. The effect on them was the reverse of joyful. Vic's face grew redder and Fynedale's whiter, and as time wore on neither of them was capable of ordinary social conversation.

Finally it worried me. All very well prospering in front of

their eyes, but when success could breed envy even in friends, in enemies it could raise spite of Himalayan proportions. Several of my new customers had transferred from Fynedale and one or two from Vic, and if I'd wanted a perfect revenge, I'd got it; but revenge was a tree with sour fruit.

Between Vic and Fynedale themselves things were no better. Under Constantine's faithful umbrella, Vic had disowned his former lieutenant and had been heard to say that if he had realized what Fynedale was up to, he would of course have had nothing to do with it. Antonia Huntercombe and the breeder of the Transporter colt would have been interested.

Probably the fact that Fynedale had two directions for hatred exhausted him to immobility. He stood about looking dazed, in a trance, as if Vic's perfidy had stunned him. He shouldn't have been so surprised, I thought. Vic always lied easily. Always had. And had always had the gift of the good liar: that people believed him.

On the Saturday afternoon, River God won the novice chase by a short head thanks entirely to Nicol's riding. I watched the triumphant unsaddling party afterward and noted that Vic was there, too, oozing bonhomie in Nicol's direction and being very man-of-the-world with Constantine. His big boyish face was back to its good-natured-looking normal, the manner easy again and confident. Kerry Sanders patted his arm and Constantine's heavy black spectacles turned repeatedly in his direction.

All sweetness and light, I thought uncharitably. Vic would always bounce back like a rubber ball.

From habit, I went to watch the next race from the jockeys' box, and Nicol climbed the steps to my side.

"Well done," I said.

"Thanks."

The runners came out onto the course and jauntily ambled down in front of the stands. Eight or nine, some of them horses I'd once ridden. I felt the usual tug of regret, of nostalgia. I wouldn't entirely get over it, I thought, until there was a completely new generation of horses. While my old partners were still running, I wanted to be on them.

Nicol said with surprised discovery, "You wish you were still riding!"

I mentally shook myself. It was no good looking back. "It's finished," I said.

"No more crashing falls. No more booing crowds. No more bloody-minded trainers telling you you rode a stinking race and engaging a different jockey next time."

"That's right."

He smiled his quick smile. "Who'd wish it on a dog?"

The runners assembled, the tapes flew up, the race went away. They were experienced hurdlers, crafty and fast, flicking over the low obstacles without altering their stride. Even though I dealt mostly with young stock for the flat, I still liked watching jumpers best.

"If I suggested to Father I would be a pro, he'd have a fit."

"Particularly," I said, "if you mentioned me in connection."

"God, yes."

The runners went down the far side and we lifted raceglasses to watch.

"Vic looks happy today," I said.

Nicol snorted. "Father told him to go to the States after Christmas and buy Kerry some colt called Phoenix Fledgling."

"With her money?"

"Why?"

"He was saying yesterday he was cutting down. So today he has a hundred thousand quid lying about loose?"

"So much?" He was surprised.

"It could be even more."

"Would Father know?" Nicol asked doubtfully.

"Vic would," I said.

Nicol shook his head. "I don't know what they're up to. Thick as thieves again today."

The runners turned in to the straight. Positions changed. The favorite came through and won smoothly, the jockey collected, expert, and totally professional.

Nicol turned to me abruptly.

"If I could ride like *that*, I'd take out a license."

"You can."

He stared. Shook his head.

"You do," I said.

Crispin had been sober since the fire. Sober and depressed.

"My life's a mess," he said.

As usual during these periods, he sat every night in my office while I got through the paperwork and did the inevitable telephoning.

"I'm going to get a job."

We both knew that he wouldn't. Those he wanted he couldn't keep. Those he could keep he despised.

"You can have one here," I said. "At this rate, I'll have to get help with the paperwork. I can't cope with it all."

"I'm not a bloody typist," he said scornfully.

"You can't type."

171

"We all know I'm absolutely useless. No need to rub it in."

"You can keep the accounts, though. You know all about figures."

He thought it over. Unreliable he might be, but not untrained. If he wanted to, he could take over the financial half of the office load and do it well.

"I'll see," he said.

Outside in the yard the demolition work was nearly finished. Plans for the new stables lay on my desk, drawn up at high speed by a local architect from the scribbled dimensions I'd given him. Depending on the time it took the Council to pass them, I'd be open for business again by the summer.

The rebuilding of the roof of the house was due to be started the following week. Rewiring from stem to stern had to be done after that, and there were several fallen ceilings to be replastered. Despite day and night oil heaters astronomicalizing my fuel bills in every room, the damp and the damp smell persisted. Repainting lay a long way ahead. It would take almost a year, I reckoned, to restore in full what had been done to intimidate me.

Vic had not seen the damage he'd caused and maybe he could put it comfortably out of his mind, but I came home to it night after night. He might forget, but he had made sure that I didn't.

Sophie had had two weeks of night shift, telling departing freight flights where to get off.

"What are you doing tomorrow?" she asked on the telephone.

"Day or night?"

"Day."

"Damn."

She laughed. "What's wrong with the day?"

"Apart from everything else . . . I have to go to Ascot Sales."

"Oh." A pause. "Couldn't I come with you?"

"If you don't mind me working."

"I'd love it. See all the little crooks doing the dirty. And Vic Vincent—will I see him?"

"I'm not taking you," I said.

"I won't bite him."

"Can't risk it."

"I promise."

When I picked her up at nine, she was still yawning from five hours' sleep and a system geared to waking at noon. She opened her door in jeans, sweater, toast, and honey.

"Come in." She gave me a slightly sticky sweet-tasting kiss. "Coffee?"

"Great."

She poured two cups in her tiny kitchen. Bright sunshine sliced through the window, giving a misleading report of the freezing day outside, where the northwest wind was doing its Arctic damnedest.

"You'll need warm boots," I said. "And sixteen layers of insulation. Also a nose muff or two and some frostbite cream."

"Think I'll stay at home and curl up with a good television program."

When wrapped up, she looked ready for Outer or even Inner Mongolia and complained that the padding made her fat.

"Ever seen a thin Eskimo?"

She tucked the blond hair away inside a fur-lined hood. "So everyone has problems."

I drove to the Ascot sale ring. Sophie's reaction, although I had forewarned her, was very much like Kerry's.

"Ascot," she said.

"At least today it isn't raining."

She huddled inside the fat-making layers. "Thank God you insisted on the igloo bit."

I took her down to the stables where there were several horses I wanted to look at; the underfoot conditions that day were rock hard, not oozing with mud. She dutifully stuck her head inside each box to look at the inmates, though her claim to know less about horses than quantum mechanics was quickly substantiated.

"Do they see two views at once, with their eyes on opposite sides of their head like that?"

"Their brains sort it out," I said.

"Very confusing."

"Most animals look sideways. And birds. And fish."

"And snakes in the grass," she said.

Some of the horses had attendants with them. Some didn't. Some had attendants who had vanished temporarily to the refreshment room. Everywhere lay the general clutter of stables in the morning: buckets, muck sacks, brushes, bandages, haynets, and halters, mostly in little clumps either outside or inside each box door. Most of the early lot numbers had stayed overnight.

I asked for three or four horses to be led out of their boxes by their attendants to get an idea of how they moved. They trotted obligingly along and back a wider piece of ground, the attendant running alongside holding them by the head on

a short rope. I watched them from behind and from dead
ahead.

"What do you look for?" Sophie said.

"Partly whether they dish their feet out sideways."

"Is that good?"

I shook my head, smiling. "The fastest ones generally
don't do it."

We went up to the O-shaped sale ring, where the wind
whistled through with enthusiasm and the meager crowd of
participants stamped their feet and tucked their hands under
their armpits. Ronnie North was there, breathing out clouds
of steam and wiping a running nose; and Vic was there,
dandified in a belted white shiny jacket with a blue shirt
underneath.

While he was deep in conversation with a client, I pointed
him out to Sophie.

"But he looks *nice*," she objected.

"Of course he does. Hundreds of people love him."

She grinned. "Such sarcasm."

I bought two three-year-old fillies for a client in Italy and
Vic watched broodingly from directly opposite.

Sophie said, "When he looks at you like that, he doesn't
look nice at all."

I took her to warm up over some coffee. It occurred to me
uneasily and belatedly that maybe I had not been clever to
bring her to Ascot. It had seemed to me that Vic was as much
interested in Sophie herself as in what I was buying, and I
wondered if he was already thinking of ways to get at me
through her.

"What's the matter?" Sophie said. "You've gone very
quiet."

"Have a doughnut?"

175

"Yes, please."

We munched and drank, and I checked ahead through the catalogue, making memory-jogging notes about the horses we had seen in their boxes.

"Does it go on like this all day?" Sophie asked.

"A bit boring for you, I'm afraid."

"No. . . . Is this what you do, day after day?"

"On sales days, yes. Other days I fix up deals privately, or go to the races, or see to things like transport and insurance. Since last week I've barely had time to cough." I told her about Wilton Young and the consequently mushrooming business.

"Are there a lot of horses for sale?" she said doubtfully. "I wouldn't have thought there were enough for so many people all to be involved in buying and selling."

"Well . . . in Britain alone there are at present about seventeen thousand thoroughbred broodmares. A mare can theoretically have a foal every year, but some years they're barren and some foals die. I suppose there must be about nine thousand new foals or yearlings on the market every season. Then there are about twenty thousand horses in training for flat races, and heaven knows how many jumpers, but more than on the flat. Horses that belong to the same people from birth to death are exceptions. Most of them change hands at least twice."

"With a commission for the agent every time?" Her expression held no approval.

I smiled. "Stockbrokers work for commission. Are they more respectable?"

"Yes."

"Why?"

"I don't know. Don't confuse me."

I said, "France, Italy, and especially America are all at it in the bloodstock business hammer and tongs. There are about thirteen hundred stud farms in the British Isles and thousands more round the world."

"All churning out horses . . . and only so that people can gamble."

I smiled at her still-disapproving expression. "Everyone needs some sort of fantasy on their bread."

She opened her mouth and shut it, and shook her head. "I can never decide whether you are very wise or an absolute fool."

"Both."

"Impossible."

"Dead easy, I'm afraid. Most people are."

We went back to the ring and watched Vic and Ronnie North beat up the price of a weedy four-year-old hurdler to twice the figure his form suggested. Vic would no doubt be collecting a sizable kickback from the seller, along with the commission from his client, and Ronnie North looked expansively pleased both with his status as underbidder for this one horse and with life in general.

Fynedale's successor, it seemed to me, had been elected.

Fynedale himself, I noticed, had arrived in the ring in time to see what was happening. He seemed to be in much the same state as before, white-faced, semi-dazed, and radiating unfocused hatred.

Sophie said, "He looks like gelignite on the boil."

"With luck he'll explode all over Vic."

"You're pretty heartless. He looks ill."

"Buzz off and mother him, then," I said.

"No, thanks."

We looked at some more horses and I bought another; we

had some more coffee and the wind blew even colder. Sophie, however, seemed content.

"Nose needs powdering," she said at one point. "Where will I meet you?"

I consulted the catalogue. "I'd better look at eighty-seven and ninety-two, in their boxes."

"O.K. I'll find you."

I looked at 87 and decided against it. Not much bone and too much white around the eye. There was no one with him. I left his box, bolted both halves of the door, and went along to 92. There I opened the top half of the door and looked inside. No attendant there either, just patient Lot 92 turning an incurious gaze. I opened the bottom half of the door and went in, letting the two halves swing shut behind me. Lot 92 was securely tied by a head-collar to a ring in the wall, but it was too cold for open doors.

The horse was a five-year-old hurdler being sold for a quick profit while he still showed promise of being useful at six. I patted his brown flank, ran my hand down his legs, and took a good close look at his teeth.

When the door opened and closed, I paid no especial attention to whatever had come in. It should have been an attendant for the horse or another like me inspecting the goods at close quarters.

It wasn't.

No instinct made me look up as I let go of the hurdler's mouth, stroked his nose, and stood back for a final appraisal.

I saw only a flash in the air. Felt the thud in my chest. And knew, falling, that the white-faced Fynedale was coming forward to finish the job.

13

He had thrown at me like a lance the most lethal of all stable equipment. A pitchfork.

The force behind his arm knocked me off my feet. I lay on my side on the straw with the two prongs embedded and the long wooden handle stretched out in front.

He could see that in spite of a deadly accurate throw and all the hate that went into it he still hadn't killed me. The glimpse I got of his distorted face convinced me that he intended to put that right.

I knew the pitchfork had gone in, but not how far. I couldn't feel much. I jerked it out and rolled over and lay on it face down, burying it under me in the straw. He fell on me, pulling, clutching, dragging, trying to get at it, and I simply lay on it like a log, not knowing what else to do.

The door opened again and light poured in from outside. Then a voice shouting. A girl's voice.

"Help! . . . Someone help!"

I knew dimly from under the flurry of Fynedale's exertions that it was Sophie. The troops she mobilized came cautiously to the rescue.

"I say," said a well-bred voice plaintively, and Fynedale took no notice.

"Here. What's going on?"

The voice, this time, was tough and the owner tougher. Hands began to pull Fynedale off me and then others to help him, and when I took my nose out of the straw I could see three men trying to hold on to Fynedale while Fynedale threw them off like pieces of hay.

He crashed out through the door with my rescuers in pursuit, and when I got from my knees to my feet the only audience was Sophie.

"Thank you," I said with feeling.

"Are you all right?"

"Yes . . . I think so."

I bent down and picked up the pitchfork.

"What's that?"

"He threw it at me," I said.

She looked at the stiletto prongs and shuddered. "Good job he missed."

"Mm." I inspected the two small tears in the front of my anorak. Then I slowly unzipped it and put a hand inside, exploring.

"He did miss, didn't he?" said Sophie, suddenly anxious.

"Direct hit. Don't know why I'm not dead."

I said it lightly and she didn't believe me, but it was the truth. I could feel the soreness of a tear in my skin and the warm stickiness of blood, but the prongs had not gone through to heart or lungs, and the force with which they'd landed had been enough to get them there.

I smiled idiotically.

"What is it?" Sophie asked.

"Thank the Lord for a dislocating shoulder. . . . The pitchfork hit the strap."

Unfortunately for Fynedale, two policemen in a patrol car had come to the sales on some unrelated errand, but when they saw three men chasing another they caught the fugitive out of habit. Sophie and I arrived to find Fynedale sitting in the police car with one policeman while the other listened to the three chasers saying that if Jonah Dereham wasn't a hospital case it was because they had saved him.

I didn't argue with that.

Sophie with unshaken composure told them about the pitchfork, and the policeman, having taken a quick look inside my anorak, told me to go and find a doctor and then come along to the local station to make a statement. I reckoned it would be the same nick I'd been to with Kerry: there would be a certain amount of doubtful eyebrow-raising over a man who got himself attacked twice in the same small sales paddock within six weeks.

At the nearest doctor's surgery the damage resolved itself into one long slit over a rib. The doctor, a girl of less than thirty, swabbed away prosaically and said that ten days earlier she'd been called to attend a farm worker who'd driven a pitchfork right through his own foot. Boot and all, she added.

I laughed. She said she hadn't meant to be funny. She had

nice legs but no sense of humor. My amusement rather died when she pointed out the state of the buckle on my strap, which she'd taken off to get at the cut. The buckle was bent. The mark of the prong showed clearly.

"One prong hit the buckle. The other went into you but slid along against a rib. I'd say you were exceptionally lucky."

I said soberly, "I'd say so, too."

She stuck on some plaster, gave me a couple of anti-infection injections, and refused my offer of a fee.

"On the National Health," she said sternly, as if offering to pay were immoral. She handed me the strap. "Why don't you get that shoulder repaired?"

"Can't spare the time . . . and I'm allergic to hospitals."

She gave my bare chest and arms a quick glance. "You've been in a few. Several of your bones have been fractured."

"Quite so," I agreed.

She allowed herself a sudden small smile. "I recognize you now. I've seen you on television. I backed your horse once in the Grand National when I was a student. I won six pounds and spent it on a book on blood diseases."

"Glad to have been of service," I said.

"I shouldn't wear that strap for a week or so," she said. "Otherwise it will rub that wound and prevent it healing."

"All right."

I thanked her for her skill, dressed, collected Sophie from the waiting room, and drifted along to the police station. Once again Sophie was offered a chair to sit on. She showed signs of exasperated patience and asked if I would be long.

"Take my car," I said contritely. "Do some shopping. Go for a walk to Windsor Park."

She considered it and brightened. "I'll come back in an hour."

The police wanted a statement from me, but I asked if I could first speak to Fynedale.

"Speak to him? Well . . . there's no law against it. He hasn't been charged yet." They shook their heads dubiously. "He's in a violent state, though. Are you sure you want to?"

"Certain."

They shrugged. "This way, then."

Fynedale was in a small bare interview room, not sitting beside the table on one of the two plain wooden chairs, but standing in the center of the largest available clear space. He vibrated still as if strung as tight as piano wire, and a muscle jumped spasmodically under his left eye.

The room, brown paint to waist height, cream above, had no windows and was lit by electric light. An impassive young policeman sat in a chair just inside the door. I asked him and the others to leave me and Fynedale to talk alone. Fynedale said loudly, "I've nothing to bloody say to you."

The policemen thought I was being foolish, but eventually they shrugged and went away.

"Sit down," I said, taking one of the chairs by the table and gesturing to the other.

"No."

"All right, don't." I pulled out cigarettes and lit one. Whatever was said about cancer of the lungs, I thought, there were times worth the risk. I drew the smoke down and was grateful for its comfort.

Fynedale began pacing around in jerky little strides.

"I *told* you I'd kill you," he said.

"Your good luck that you didn't."

He stopped dead. "What did you say?"

"If you had, you'd have spent ten years inside."

"Bloody worth it." He went back to pacing.

"I see Vic's got another partner," I said.

He picked up a chair and threw it viciously against the wall. The door opened immediately and the young policeman stepped hurriedly in.

"Please wait," I said. "We've hardly started."

He looked indecisively at Fynedale, the fallen chair, and me sitting calmly smoking, and decided that perhaps after all it would be safe to leave. The door closed quietly behind him.

"Vic's done the dirty on you, I reckon," I said.

He circled behind me. The hairs on my neck bristled. I took another lungful of smoke and didn't look round.

"Getting you into trouble and then ditching you."

"It was you got me into trouble." The voice was a growl in the throat.

I knew that any tenseness in my body would react on him and screw him up even tighter, but it took a fair amount of concentration to relax every muscle with him out of sight behind my head. I tried to make my voice slow, thoughtful, persuasive, but my mouth was as dry as a Sunday in Salt Lake City.

"Vic started it," I said. "Vic and you. Now it's Vic and Ronnie North. You and I—we've both come off worst with Vic. . . ."

He reappeared jerkily into my field of vision. The carrot hair looked bright orange under the electric bulb. His eyes alternately shone with manic fire when the light caught them and receded into secretive shadows when he bent his head. Sophie's remarks about gelignite on the boil came back to me; and his instability had, if anything, increased.

"Cigarette?" I suggested.

"Get stuffed."

It was better when I could see him.

I said, "What have you told the police?"

"Nothing. Bloody nothing."

"Did they get you to make a statement?"

"That they bloody did not."

"Good," I said. "That simplifies things."

"What the hell are you on about?"

I watched the violence and agitation in every physical movement. It was as if his muscles and nerves were acting in spasms, as if some central disorganization were plucking wires.

I said, "What is upsetting you most?"

"Most?" he yelled. "Most? The fact that you're bloody walking in here as cool as bloody cucumbers, that's what. I tried to kill you. *Kill you!*"

He stopped as if he couldn't explain what he meant, but he'd got his message across to me loud and clear. He had taken himself beyond the edge of sense in his compulsion to do me harm, and there I was, proving that it had all been for nothing. I guessed that he badly needed not to have failed entirely. I took off my jacket and explained about the strap and buckle saving my life. I undid my shirt, showed him the plaster, and told him what lay underneath.

"It hurts," I said truthfully.

He stopped pacing and peered closely at my face. "Does it?"

"Yes."

He put out his hand and touched me. I winced.

He stood back, bent and picked up the chair he'd thrown, set it on its feet on the far side of the table, and sat down opposite me. He stretched for the packet of cigarettes and the lighter, which I'd left lying, and lit one with hands still shaking with tension.

I left my shirt undone and falling open. He sat smoking jerkily, his eyes flicking every few seconds to the strip of plaster. It seemed to satisfy him. To reassure. Finally to soothe. He smoked the whole cigarette through without speaking, but the jerky movements gradually quieted, and by the time he threw the stub on the floor and twisted his foot on it the worst of the jangle had disappeared.

"I'll make a bargain with you," I said.

"What bargain?"

"I'll say the pitchfork was an accident."

"You know bloody well it wasn't."

"I know. You know. The police know. But there were no witnesses. . . . If I swear it was an accident, there would be no question of you being even charged with attempted murder, let alone tried and convicted."

He thought it over. There were a lot of little twitches in the muscles of his face, and the skin stretched gauntly over the cheekbones.

"You don't actually want to do time, do you?" I said.

"No."

"Suppose we could get you off all the hooks. . . . Assault, fraud—the lot."

"You couldn't."

"I could keep you out of jail, that's for sure."

A long pause. Then he said, "A bargain. That means you want something in return."

"Mm."

"What, then?"

I ran my tongue round my teeth and took my time over replying.

"I want," I said slowly, "I want you to talk about the way you and Vic tried to make me join your ring."

He was surprised. "Is that all?"

"It'll do for a start."

"But you know. You know what Vic said to you."

"I don't know what he said to *you*."

He shrugged in bewilderment. "He just said if you wouldn't go along with us, we'd break you."

"Look," I said, "the price of your freedom is every word, every scrap of conversation that you can remember. Especially everything about that ally of Vic's who got my stable burned."

"I told you. . . . I don't know."

"If you want to get out of here, you're going to have to do better than that."

He stared across the table. I saw his understanding of my offer deepen. He looked briefly round the bleak crowding walls of the little interview room and shivered. The last vestiges of the exalted murderous state evaporated. He looked smaller and colder and no danger to anybody.

"All right," he said. "I reckon I don't owe Vic much any more. I'll not go to jail just to save his bloody skin. I'll tell you what I can."

It took three more cigarettes and a lot of pauses, but he did his best.

"I reckon it started about six weeks ago. I mean, for some time before that Vic had said a few things about you being the biggest danger on the horizon. You were pretty good as an agent and dead honest, and he thought you might drain off some of the business that he'd otherwise corner."

"Room for us all," I murmured.

"Not what Vic thought. Anyway, about six weeks ago he said it was time to bust you once and for all." He thought for a while, sucking deep on his cigarette. "See, Vic and I and some of the others had this thing going—"

"The kickback system," I said.

"Aye. All right, so goody-goody sods like you can look down their noses and sniff, but it's not illegal and it does a lot of people a lot of bloody good."

"Some people."

"All right, so the client pays over the odds, so what? Anyway, as Vic always says, the higher the prices the more commission the auctioneers get and the better they like it, so they're just as bad, running things up as far as they bloody can."

They also had a duty to the seller, I thought, but it wasn't the time to argue.

"Well, there we were, running this little ring and doing better and better out of it, and then one day—I suppose it was just before the first yearling sales at Newmarket. . . ." He paused, looking back in his mind. His voice died away.

"What happened?" I prompted.

"Vic was sort of—I don't know—excited and scared, both at once."

"Vic was scared?" I said skeptically

"Aye, he was. Sort of. Sort of excited, though. Like someone had put him up to something he wanted to do but knew he shouldn't."

"Like stealing apples?"

He brushed off the childish parallel. "These were no apples. Vic said we'd make so much money that what had gone before was only peanuts. He said there was a deal we could do with a breeder that had a colt by Transporter that was a perfect peach—''

"Was it Vic's own idea?" I asked.

"I thought so. . . . I don't know. . . . Anyway, it worked a dream. He gave me five thousand quid just for bidding, and he made twenty out of it himself."

"By my reckoning he made thirty."

"Oh, no." He stopped, surprised, then went on more slowly. "No . . . I remember him saying . . . ten thousand pounds went to the bloke who wrote the agreement that Vic got the breeder to sign. I said I thought it was a lot, but Vic says you have to pay for expert advice."

"Does he often pay for expert advice?"

He nodded. "All the time."

"Cheerfully?"

"What? Of course."

"He isn't being blackmailed?"

He looked scornful. "I'll say not. You can't see any piddling little blackmailer putting one over on Vic."

"No . . . But what it amounts to is that Vic was collecting huge kickbacks from breeders and other vendors, and out of that he was paying his own kickbacks to someone else for expert advice."

He frowned. "I suppose you could say so."

"But you don't know who?"

"No."

"How long would you say he has been receiving this advice?"

"How the hell do I know? A year. Two. About that."

"So what was different about the last six weeks?"

"You were. All of a sudden Vic says it's time to get rid of you. Either that or make you back down and take your cut with the rest of us. We all thought you'd come in with us with a bit of pressure. Well, see, it didn't make sense you holding out. Only do yourself a lot of harm. Jiminy Bell, he says now he told us you'd never agree, but he bloody didn't. That little sod, he said then that you were pretty soft really. A soft touch, he always said. Always good for a sob story. So now he says he told us you were a tough nut, the squirmy little liar.''

"Does Vic see this friend of his every day?"

"Couldn't say."

"Well . . . think."

He thought. "I'd say that most days he either sees him or talks on the phone. See, Vic always gets things done quickly, like pinching that horse you bought at Ascot. . . ."

"How was that done?"

He blinked. Shifted uneasily on his chair. I shoved the cigarettes across and tried to look as if the whole question were quite impersonal.

"Er . . ." he said. "Vic said you were buying a horse for Mrs. Sanders and he couldn't have that; she was marrying Constantine Brevett and he was Vic's exclusive territory."

"When did he say that?"

"At the sales the day you bought Hearse Puller."

"Had he already fixed up with Fred Smith?"

He hesitated. "He knew Fred Smith was going to take away whatever horse you bought. Yes."

"Did Vic himself fix it with Fred Smith?"

"See, I don't really know. Vic said he didn't, but I don't know; he'd say his grandmother was a pygmy if it suited him."

"Ronnie North," I said slowly. "Did he know Fred Smith?"

Fynedale's face twisted into a sardonic sneer. "Old mates, weren't they?"

"Were they?"

"Well . . . Ronnie, he came from Stepney way, same as Fred Smith. Ronnie started in the horse-coping business in the old days when they sold horses on market days in all the big towns. He started as a boy, helping his dad. Bloody lot of gypsies, if you ask me. Up to every damn trick in the book, is Ronnie. But bright, see? Got brains, Ronnie has."

"Ronnie sold me the next horse I bought for Kerry Sanders."

"Aye. Him and Vic, laughing themselves sick about it, they were. Then Ronnie afterwards said you needed a bloody lesson, busting Fred Smith's arm."

"Did you yourself ever meet Fred Smith?"

"I saw him, like. Saw him at Ascot, with Ronnie. Ronnie pointed you out to him. We all did, see?"

"I see."

"Then, well, with River God it was dead easy, wasn't it? Ronnie found which transport firm you'd engaged and got them to tell him their instructions, and he just sent Fred Smith to pick you off on the lay-by."

"Ronnie sent him?"

"Ronnie . . . or Vic." He shrugged. "One of them."

"Not Vic's unknown friend?"

"Might have been, I suppose." He didn't think it made much difference. "We weren't going to steal River God, see? Fred Smith had the money for it. He was going to make you take it, like at Ascot."

"And River God was going back to Ronnie North?"

"Aye."

"Then why did he agree to sell it to me in the first place?"

He said with exaggerated patience, as if talking to a dim child, "See, he wasn't going to, first off. Then he rings Vic and says you're looking for another horse instead of Hearse Puller. Then Vic rings back and says sell you River God and it'll be a good opportunity of bashing you up a bit more."

"Did you actually hear either of these calls?"

"Eh?" He shook his head. "I don't live in Vic's pocket, do I? No, Vic told me."

I thought for a while. "All right," I said, "which of you thought of burning my yard?"

He shifted his chair abruptly so that he was no longer facing me, but spoke to the bare walls.

"See . . . Vic said . . . a real smash and you'd cave in. See . . . he saw you talking to that Transporter breeder—and that trainer whose owner he'd swiped—in the bar, see?"

"Yes."

"Aye. Well, then, Vic says this time no messing, you've got to be put right out of action, because this expert friend of his has thought up a fiddle to make the Transporter colt look like hayseeds, only he wouldn't tell Vic what it was while you were still around at the sales. Vic said this expert was afraid you would make a public fuss, which would mean everyone would be a lot more careful about buying horses in the future and that was the last thing they wanted. So Vic said you either had to join in or be got rid of and you'd made it crystal clear you wouldn't join in, so it was your own bloody fault you got your yard burned."

I grunted. "And what happened afterwards?"

"Well, there you bloody were at the sales as if nothing had happened. The whole thing had been a flop and Fred Smith was in jail and Vic was furious because he couldn't start the new fiddle. He said he'd just have to go on with the kickbacks, and anyway we'd been doing pretty well out of those for two years so it didn't seem too bad.''

He swung round again, his face full of renewed anger.

''And then you had to bugger the whole thing up by ratting to Wilton Young.''

''Calm down,'' I said flatly. ''Did you expect me to go on meekly taking whatever you cared to dish out?''

He looked indecisive. ''Don't know.''

You know now, I thought.

''Are Vic and his expert friend still planning this new big fiddle for some time in the future?''

''Aye. They are. Today. . . . Today?'' He seemed suddenly astounded that it was only that morning that he had gone to Ascot Sales.

''Today . . . I could have killed Vic. I told him I could kill him—and kill you, too—and he said why didn't I just kill you, then he could get on with the fiddle. And he was bloody laughing—but I reckon now he meant to egg me on.''

''I expect he did,'' I said.

''Aye. He'd be rid of you and me, too. He'd have the whole bloody field to himself.''

He leaned his elbows on the table and picked up my lighter and fidgeted with it.

''Here,'' he said. ''I'll tell you something. You can put Vic in the same boat as you did me.''

''Do you mean . . . had up for fraud?''

''Aye . . . Makes shipping horses by sea instead of air look like kids' stuff.''

''Tell me, then.''

He looked up. ''You meant it straight, didn't you, about getting me out of here?''

''I did.''

He sighed. "Reckon I can trust you. And that's a bloody laugh, for a start."

He threw down the lighter and leaned back.

"Right, then," he said. "Vic swindled the High Power Insurance Company out of a hundred and fifteen thousand quid."

14

£

"Are you sure?" I said.

"Positive."

"Can you prove it?"

"I reckon *you* could, if you wanted to."

"How did he do it?"

"See . . . it was about three years ago. He shipped a four-year-old stallion out to Japan. Polyprint, it was called."

I said, "I remember that. It died on the way."

"Aye. It did. And Vic had insured it for a hundred and fifteen thousand for the journey, with himself to collect if anything happened to the horse."

"Nothing especially unusual in that."

"No. And he insured it a week before it was due to go.

That is what made the insurance firm pay up. Because a week before the horse set off, Vic couldn't have known it was going to die, because a vet had been over it from nose to arse and given it the O.K., and it was the High Power Company's own vet, which strung them up proper.''

"I can't remember what it died of."

"Tetanus," he said. "Three days by air to Japan. They took it out of Gatwick looking as right as rain. . . . It walked up the ramp into the aircraft as quiet as you please. By the time they got to the Middle East, it was sweating something chronic. Next stop, they got it out and walked it around, but it was staggering a bit. Next stop they had a local vet waiting. Tetanus, he said. So they cabled the insurance company and they wanted to send their own man out to take a look. See, there was a lot of brass involved. Anyway he never went, because the horse died while the man was still in England getting cholera jabs or something. So Vic claims the money, and the High Power has to pay up.''

"Did Vic travel with the horse himself?"

"No. He was right here in England."

"So . . . where was the fraud?"

"Ah. . . . See, the horse that set off for Japan and died of tetanus, that horse wasn't Polyprint.''

He lit a cigarette, absorbed in his story.

"It was a horse called Nestegg."

I stared at him. "Nestegg is standing at stud in Ireland."

"Aye," he said. "And that's Polyprint."

The gaunt face twisted into the ghost of a smile. "See, Vic bought Nestegg because he had a client who wanted it. Nestegg was six and had won a few long-distance races, and this client had a small stud and wanted a stallion that wouldn't cost too much. Well, Vic bought Nestegg for ten thousand and was going to pass him on for fifteen, and then this client just dropped down dead one afternoon and the widow said nothing doing she didn't want to know. Vic wasn't much worried, because Nestegg wasn't bad, really.''

He took a few deep puffs, sorting things out.

"One evening I was at Vic's place near Epsom and we looked round the yard, like one does. He shows me Polyprint, who's due to set off to Japan the next day. Big bay horse. Full of himself. Then, three boxes along, there was Nestegg. Another bay, much the same. We went in and looked at him and he was standing there all hunched up and sweating. Vic looked him over and said he would go out and see him again later, and if he was no better he would get the vet in the morning. Then we went into Vic's house for a drink, and then I went home.''

He looked at me broodingly.

"So the next day off goes this horse to Japan and dies of tetanus two days later. Next time I saw Vic, he sort of winks at me and gives me a thousand quid in readies, and I laughed and took it. Then later he sold this bay he still had, which was supposed to be Nestegg but was really Polyprint. He sold him to a stud in Ireland for seventeen thousand. He wouldn't have made a penny if he'd sent Polyprint off to Japan and got a vet to try to save Nestegg. Just by swapping those two horses when he had the chance, he made himself a proper packet.''

"And it gave him a taste for more easy money in large amounts?''

"Aye. . . . It was after that that he latched on to the kickbacks in a big way. He asked me to help. . . . Tell you the truth, I was glad to.''

"And he found this expert," I said.

"Aye. . . ." He hesitated. "It was maybe the other way round. Vic more or less said this chap had come to him and suggested more ways Vic could make money."

"He hadn't done so badly on his own," I observed.

"Well . . . Polyprint was a one-off, see. You couldn't work that again. He only did it because he realized Nestegg had tetanus and would die pretty quickly if he wasn't treated and even maybe if he was. See, tetanus isn't that common. You couldn't have two die of it on journeys when they were heavily insured, even if you could infect them on purpose, which you can't. Vic walked that horse around all night to keep it moving and fed it a bucketful of tranquilizers so that it looked all right when it was loaded on the plane at Gatwick. But to get another one to die on a journey you'd have to fix some sort of accident. The insurance people would be dead suspicious, and even if they paid up they might afterwards refuse to insure you altogether and you couldn't risk that, see. But the thing about this expert chap was that nearly everything he suggested was legal. Vic said it was like property development and land speculation. You could make a great deal of money without breaking the law if you knew how to set about it."

The police were understandably sour about my assertion that I had fallen on the pitchfork by accident and that Fynedale was as innocent of assault as a bunch of violets. They argued and I insisted, and half an hour later Fynedale stood outside on the pavement shivering in the wind.

"Thanks," he said briefly. He looked shrunken and depressed.

He huddled inside his jacket, turned on his heel, and

walked away up the street to the railway station. The red hair was a receding blob against the dead copper leaves of a beech hedge.

Sophie was waiting by the curb, sitting in the driving seat of my car. I opened the passenger-side door and slid in beside her.

"Will you drive?" I said.

"If you like."

I nodded.

"You look bushed," she said. She started the engine, shifted the gears, and edged out into the road.

"Couldn't beat Muhammad Ali right now."

She smiled. "How did it go?"

"Like a torrent, once he'd started."

"What did you learn?"

I thought, trying to put everything into its right order. Sophie drove carefully, flicking glances across, waiting for an answer.

I said, "Vic swindled an insurance company very neatly, about three years ago. Some time after that, someone who Fynedale calls an expert sought Vic out and suggested a sort of alliance, in which Vic would extort money in various more or less legal ways and pay a proportion of it to the expert. I imagine this expert guessed Vic had swindled the insurance and was therefore a good prospect for a whole career of legal robbery."

"There's no such thing as legal robbery."

I smiled. "How about wealth taxes?"

"That's different."

"Taking by law is legal robbery."

"Ah, well—go on about Vic."

"Vic and the expert started redistributing wealth in no

uncertain terms, chiefly into their own pockets but with enough pickings to entice six or seven other agents into the ring.''

''Fynedale?'' Sophie said.

''Yes. Especially Fynedale, as he knew about the original insurance swindle. It just seems to have been my bad luck that I started being an agent at about the time Vic and the expert were warming things up. Pauli Teksa had a theory that Vic and his friends wanted me out of the way because I was a threat to their monopoly, and from what Fynedale says I should think he might have been right, though I thought it was nonsense when he suggested it.''

I yawned. Sophie drove smoothly, as controlled at the wheel as everywhere else. She had taken off the fur-lined hood, and the silver-blond hair fell gently to her shoulders. Her profile was calm, efficient, content. I thought that probably I did love her, and would for a long time. I also guessed that however often I might ask her to marry me, in the end she would not. The longer and better I knew her, the more I realized that she was by nature truly solitary. Lovers she might take, but a bustling family life would be alien and disruptive. I understood why her four years with the pilot had been a success: it was because of his continual long absences, not in spite of them. I understood her lack of even the memory of inconsolable grief. His death had merely left her where she basically liked to be, which was alone.

''Go on about Vic,'' she said.

''Oh . . . well . . . They started this campaign of harassment. Compulsive purchase of Hearse Puller at Ascot. Sending Fred Smith down to my place to do what harm he could, which turned out to be giving Crispin whiskey and letting loose that road-hogging two-year-old. Arranging for me to buy and lose River God. When all that—and a few bits of intimidation from Vic himself—failed to work, they reckoned that burning my stable would do the trick.''

"Their mistake.''

"Yeah . . . well . . . they did it.'' I yawned again. "Fred Smith, now. Vic and the expert needed some muscle. Ronnie North knew Fred Smith. Vic must have asked Ronnie if he knew anyone suitable and Ronnie suggested Fred Smith.''

"Bingo.''

"Mm. . . . You know something odd?''

"What?''

"The insurance company that Vic swindled was the one Crispin used to work for.''

Sophie made us tea in her flat. We sat side by side on the sofa, bodies casually touching in intimate friendship, sipping the hot reviving liquid.

"I ought to sleep a bit,'' she said. "I'm on duty at eight.''

I looked at my watch. Four-thirty, and darkening already toward the winter night. It had seemed a long day.

"Shall I go?''

She smiled. "Depends how sore you are.''

"Sex is a great anesthetic.''

"Nuts.''

We went to bed and put it fairly gently to the test, and certainly what I felt most was not the stab along my rib.

The pattern as before: sweet, intense, lingering, a vibration of subtle pleasure from head to foot. She breathed softly and slowly and smiled with her eyes, as close as my soul and as private as her own.

Eventually she said sleepily, "Do you always give girls what suits them best?''

I yawned contentedly. "What suits them best is best for me."

"The voice of experience . . ." She smiled drowsily, drifting away.

We woke to the clatter of her alarm less than two hours later. She stretched out a hand to shut it off, then rolled her head over on the pillow for a kiss.

"Better than sleeping pills," she said. "I feel as if I'd slept all night."

She made coffee and rapid bacon and eggs, because to her it seemed time for breakfast, and in an organized hurry she offered her cheek in goodbye on the pavement and drove away to work.

I watched her rear lights out of sight. I remembered I had read somewhere that air-traffic controllers had the highest divorce rates on earth.

Wilton Young came to Cheltenham races the following day in spite of the basic contempt he held for steeplechasing because of its endemic shortage of brass. He came because the rival tycoon who was sponsoring the day's big race had asked him, and the first person he saw at the pre-lunch reception was me.

"What are you doing here?" he said bluntly.

"I was invited."

"Oh."

He didn't quite ask why, so I told him. "I rode a few winners for our host."

He cast his mind back and gave a sudden remembering nod. "Aye. So you did."

A waiter offered a silver tray with glasses of champagne. Wilton Young took one, tasted it with a grimace, and said he would tell me straight he would sooner have had a pint of bitter.

"I'm afraid I may have some disappointing news for you," I said.

He immediately looked belligerent. "Exactly what?"

"About Fynedale."

"Him!" His eyes narrowed. "Any bad news about him is good news."

I said, "The man I sent to South Africa says he can't swear the extra horses he looked after on the way were yours."

"You seemed sure enough that he would."

"He says he had the impression they were yours, but he couldn't be sure."

"That'll not stand up in court."

"No."

He grunted. "I'll not sue, then. I'll not throw good brass after bad. Suing's a mug's game where there's any doubt."

His plain honesty rebuked me for the lie I'd told him. My man had been absolutely positive about the horses' ownership: he'd seen the papers. I reckoned my promise to get Fynedale off was fully discharged and from there on he would have to take his chances.

"What's past is past," Wilton Young said. "Cut your losses. Eh, lad?"

"I guess so," I said.

"Take my word for it. Now, look here. I've a mind to buy an American horse. Tough, that's what they are. Tough as if they came from Yorkshire." He wasn't joking. "There's one particular one I want you to go and buy for me. He comes up for sale soon after Christmas."

I stared at him, already guessing.

"Phoenix Fledgling. A two-year-old. Ever heard of it?"

"Did you know," I said, "that Constantine Brevett is after it, too?"

He chuckled loudly. "Why the hell do you think I want it? Put his bloody superior nose out of joint. Eh, lad?"

The bloody superior nose chose that precise moment to arrive at the reception, closely accompanied by the firm mouth, smooth gray hair, black-framed spectacles, and general air of having come straight from some high-up chairmanship in the City.

As his height and booming voice instantly dominated the assembly, I reflected that the advantage always seemed to go to the one who arrived later: maybe if Constantine and Wilton Young both realized it, they would try so hard to arrive after each other that neither would appear at all, which might be a good idea all round. Constantine's gaze swept authoritatively over the guests and stopped abruptly on Wilton Young and me. He frowned very slightly. His mouth marginally compressed. He gave us five seconds' uninterrupted attention, and then looked away.

"Has it ever occurred to you," I said slowly, "that it might just be *your* nose that *he's* putting out of joint?"

"Don't be daft."

"How many times have you had to outbid him to get a horse?"

He chuckled. "Can't remember. I've beaten him more times than he's sold office blocks."

"He's cost you a great deal of money."

The chuckle died. "That was bloody Fynedale and Vic Vincent."

"But . . . what if Constantine approved—or even planned it?"

"You're chasing the wrong rabbit, I tell thee straight."

I chewed my lower lip. "As long as you're happy."

"Aye."

Nicol won the amateurs' race by some startlingly aggressive tactics that wrung obscenities from his opponents and some sharp-eyed looks from the Stewards. He joined me afterward with defiance flying like banners.

"How about that, then?" he said, attacking first.

"If you were a pro on the flat, you'd have been suspended."

"That's right."

"A proper sportsman," I said dryly.

"I'm not in it for the sport."

"What, then?"

"Winning."

"Just like Wilton Young," I said.

"What do you mean?"

"Neither of you cares what winning costs."

He glared. "It cost you enough in your time in smashed-up bones."

"Well . . . maybe everyone pays in the way that matters to them least."

"I don't give a damn what the others think of me."

"That's what I mean."

We stood in silence, watching horses go by. All my life I'd stood and watched horses go by. There were a lot worse ways of living.

"When you grow up," I said, "you'll be a bloody good jockey."

"You absolute sod." The fury of all his twenty-two pampered years bunched into fists. Then, with the speed of all his mercurial changes, he gave me instead the brief, flashing, sardonic smile. "O.K. O.K. *O.K.* I just aged five years."

He turned on his heel and strode away, and although I didn't know it until afterward, he walked straight into the Clerk of the Course's office and filled out an application form for a license.

Vic didn't come to Cheltenham races. I had business with him, however, so after a certain amount of private homework I drove to his place near Epsom early on the following morning.

He lived as he dressed, a mixture of distinguished traditional and flashy modern. The house, down a short well-kept drive off a country by-road on the outskirts of Oxshott Woods, had at heart the classically simple lines of early-Victorian stone. Stuck on the back was an Edwardian outcrop of kitchens and bathrooms and to one side sprawled an extensive new single-story wing that proved to embrace a swimming pool, a garden room, and a suite for guests.

Vic was in his stables, a brick-built quadrangle standing apart from the house. He came out of its archway, saw me standing by my car, and walked across with no welcome written plain on his large unsmiling face.

"What the hell do you want?" he said.

"To talk to you."

The cold sky was thick with clouds and the first heavy drops spoke of downpours to come. Vic looked irritated and said he had nothing to say.

"I have," I said.

It began to rain in earnest. Vic turned on his heel and hurried away toward the house, and I followed him closely. He was even more irritated to find me going in with him through his own door.

"I've nothing to say," he repeated.

"You'll listen, then."

We stood in a wide passage running between the old part of the house and the new, with central heating rushing out past us into the chilly air of Surrey. Vic tightened his mouth, shut the outer door, and jerked his head for me to follow.

Money had nowhere been spared. Large expanses of pale blue carpeting stretched to the horizon. Huge plushy sofas stood round. Green plants the size of saplings sprouted from Greek-looking pots. He probably had a moon bath, I thought, with gold taps, and a water bed for sleep.

I remembered the holes in Antonia Huntercombe's ancient chintz. Vic's legal robbery had gone a long way too far.

He took me to the room at the far end of the hallway, his equivalent of my office. From there the one window looked out to the pool, with the guest rooms to the left, and the garden room to the right. His rows of record books were much like mine, but there ended the resemblance between the two rooms. His had bright new paint, pale blue carpet, three or four Florentine mirrors, Bang and Olufsen stereo, and a well-stocked bar.

"Right," Vic said. "Get it over. I've no time to waste."

"Ever heard of a horse called Polyprint?" I said.

He froze. For countable seconds not a muscle twitched. Then he blinked.

"Of course."

"Died of tetanus."

"Yes."

"Ever heard of Nestegg?"

If I'd run him through with a knitting needle, he would have been no more surprised. The stab went through him visibly. He didn't answer.

"When Nestegg was foaled," I said conversationally,

"there was some doubt as to his paternity. One of two stallions could have covered the dam. So the breeder had Nestegg's blood typed."

Vic gave a great imitation of Lot's wife.

"Nestegg's blood was found to be compatible with one of the stallions, but not with the other. Records were kept. Those records still exist."

No sign.

"A full brother of Polyprint is now in training in Newmarket."

Nothing.

I said, "I have arranged a blood test for the horse now known as Nestegg. You and I both know that his blood type will be entirely different from that recorded for Nestegg as a foal. I have also arranged a blood test for Polyprint's full brother. And his blood type will be entirely compatible with the one found in the supposed Nestegg."

"You *bugger*." The words exploded from him, all the more forceful for his unnatural immobility.

"On the other hand," I said, "the tests have not yet been made, and in certain circumstances I would cancel them."

His breath came back. He moved. "What circumstances?" he said.

"I want an introduction."

"A what?"

"To a friend of yours. The friend who drew up the agreement that the breeder of the Transporter colt signed. The friend who decided to burn my stable."

Vic moved restlessly.

"Impossible."

I said without heat, "It's either that or I write to the High Power Insurance people."

He fidgeted tensely with some pens lying on his desk.

"What would you do if you met . . . this friend?"

"Negotiate for permanent peace."

He picked up a calendar, looked at it unseeingly, and put it down.

"Today's Saturday," I said. "The blood tests are scheduled for Monday morning. If I meet your friend today or tomorrow, I'll call them off."

He was more furious than frightened, but he knew as well as I did that those blood tests would be his first step to the dock. What I didn't know was whether Vic, like Fred Smith, would swallow the medicine with, so to speak, his mouth shut.

Vic said forcefully, "You'd always have that threat over me. It's bloody blackmail."

"Sort of," I agreed.

Ripples of resentment screwed up his face. I watched him searching for a way out.

"Face-to-face with your friend," I said. "Five minutes will do. That's not much when you think what you stand to lose if I don't get it." I gestured round his bright room and out to the luxurious pool. "Built on Polyprint's insurance, no doubt."

He banged his fist down on the desk, making the pens rattle.

"Bloody Fynedale told you," he shouted. "It must have been. I'll murder the little rat!"

I didn't exactly deny it, but instead I said matter-of-factly, "One calculation you left out: my brother Crispin worked for High Power."

15

£

Crispin stood in the yard at home looking miserable and broody. I stopped the car on my return from Vic's and climbed out to meet him.

"What's the matter?" I said.

"Oh . . ." He swung an arm wide in frustration, indicating the flattened stable area and the new scaffolding climbing up to the burnt part of the roof.

"All this . . . If I hadn't been drunk, it wouldn't have happened."

I looked at him. "Don't worry about it."

"But I do. If I'd been around. . . . If there had been lights on in the house, that man wouldn't have set fire—"

"You don't know that he wouldn't," I said.

"Stands to reason."

"No. Come on in, it's cold out here."

We went into the kitchen and I made coffee. Crispin's mood of self-abasement flickered on fitfully while he watched me put the water and coffee into the percolator.

"It would have been better if you had let me die."

"It was a good job you passed out in the bathroom," I said. "It was the only room that had natural ventilation through an air-brick."

He wasn't cheered. "Better if I'd snuffed it."

"Want some toast?"

"Stop bloody talking about food. I'm saying you should have let me die."

"I know you are. It's damn silly. I don't want you dead. I want you alive and well and living in Surrey."

"You don't take me seriously." His voice was full of injured complaint.

I thought of all the other conversations we'd had along those lines. I ought to have let him drown in the bath the time he went to sleep there. I ought to have let him drive into a tree the time I'd taken his car keys away. I ought to have let him fall off the Brighton cliffs the time he tottered dizzily to the edge.

Blaming me for not letting him die was his way of laying all his troubles at my door. It was my fault he was alive, his mind went, so it was my fault if he took refuge in drink. He would work up his resentment against me as a justification for self-pity.

I sighed inwardly and made the toast. Either that day or the next, he would be afloat again on gin.

There was no word from Vic. I spent all day working in

the office and watching racing on television, with Crispin doing his best to put his mind to my accounts.

"When you worked for High Power," I said, "did you have anything to do with a claim for a horse called Polyprint?"

He sniffed. "You know damn well I was in Pensions, not Claims."

"Just thought you might have heard . . ."

"No."

We drank Coke and fizzy lemonade and coffee, and I grilled some lamb chops for supper, and still Vic didn't telephone.

Same thing the next morning. Too much silence. I bit my nails and wondered what to do if my lever didn't work; if Vic wouldn't tell and the friend wouldn't save him. The blood-type tests could go ahead and chop Vic into little pieces, but the friend would be free and undiscovered and could recruit another lieutenant and start all over again, like cancer.

I wandered round the place where the stable had been, desultorily kicking at loose stones.

A car turned into the yard, one I didn't know, and from it stepped a total stranger. Tall, young, blond. Surely this couldn't be Vic's friend, I thought, and it wasn't. There were two other people in the car with him, and from the back of it stepped Sophie.

"Hi . . ." She grinned at my face. "Who were you expecting? The bailiffs?"

She introduced the friends, Peter and Sue. They were all on their way to lunch with Sue's parents, but if I liked she could stop off with me and they would pick her up on their way back.

212

I liked. The friends waved and went, and Sophie tucked her arm through mine.

"How about marriage?" I said.

"No."

"Why not?"

"Because you like oysters and I don't."

I smiled and steered her into the house. It was as good an answer as any.

Crispin was highly restless, and not in the least pleased to see her.

"I'll go for a walk," he said. "I can see I'm not wanted."

"You'll stay right where you are and pour us some Cokes." I said firmly. We looked at each other, both knowing that if he went for a walk it would lead to the pub.

"All right," he said abruptly. "You bloody bully."

I cooked the lunch: steaks and grilled tomatoes. Crispin said that Sophie ought to do it and Sophie said you should never interfere in someone else's kitchen. They looked at each other with unfriendly eyes, as if each wished that the other weren't there. Not the most relaxed of Sunday lunch parties, I thought; and Vic telephoned with the coffee.

"My friend will meet you," he said. "For five minutes only. Like you said."

"Where?" I asked.

"Here. At my house. Six o'clock."

"I'll be there," I said.

His voice held a mixture of instructions and anxiety. "You'll cancel those blood tests?"

"Yeah," I said. "After the meeting, I will."

I went back to the kitchen. Sophie was smoking and Crispin glowered at his coffee as if it were an enemy. When we were alone, he often stacked the plates in the dishwasher

213

but I knew he wouldn't do it while she was there. He took it for granted that if there was a woman in the room she would do the household chores, even if she was a guest. Sophie saw no reason to do jobs she disliked—and her host's jobs, at that—simply because she was female. I watched the two of them with a sad sort of amusement, my liability of a brother and the girl who wouldn't be my wife.

During the afternoon, Peter and Sue rang to say they were staying overnight with Sue's parents and consequently couldn't take Sophie home. Would I mind frightfully driving her home myself?

I explained to Sophie that I had an appointment near Epsom.

"That's all right," she said. "I'll wait in the car while you do your business, and we can go on to my place after."

A flicker of caution made me uneasy. "I'm going to see Vic Vincent," I said.

"Is he likely to be as lethal as Fynedale?"

I smiled. "No."

"And don't forget it was a good job I was with you at Ascot."

"I haven't."

"Well, then."

So I took her.

Crispin followed us out to the car. "I suppose you won't be back till bloody morning," he said.

"Whether I am or not, you'll be all right."

He looked at me in desperation. "You know I bloody won't."

"You can be if you want to," I said persuasively.

"Sod you, Jonah."

He stood and watched us as I started the car and drove

away. As usual, he had made me feel a grinding guilt at leaving him to struggle alone. As usual, I told myself that if he was ever to beat the drink he would have to stay off it when I wasn't there. I simply couldn't be beside him every minute of his life.

We drove toward Epsom. We were early, by design. Vic had said six o'clock, but I thought that a preliminary scout around might be prudent. The friend, whoever he was, had already sent a load of trouble my way, and I had a minimum of faith that all would henceforth be caviar and handshakes.

I drove fifty yards past the entrance to Vic's drive, and pulled up on the grass verge with Sophie's door pressed close against the hedge. I switched off the lights and turned to her.

"When I go, lock my door behind me," I said. "And don't get out of the car."

"Jonah. . . . You really do think Vic might be lethal."

"Not Vic. But he might have someone else with him. . . . I don't know. Anyway, I'll be much happier if I'm sure you're sitting here snug and safe."

"But . . ."

"No buts." I kissed her lightly. "I'll be back in half an hour or so. If I'm not here by six-thirty, drive on into Epsom and raise a posse."

"I don't like it."

"Put the rug round you or you'll get cold."

I slid out of the car and watched her lock the door. Waved. Smiled as if I were going to the circus. Went away.

The night was not pitch dark. Few nights are. My eyes adjusted to the dimness and I went quietly through the gateway and up alongside the drive, walking on the grass. I had worn for the occasion a black sweater and dark trousers, black rubbersoled shoes. I pulled a pair of gloves from my pocket and put them on. I have dark brown hair, which helped, and apart from the pale blob of my face I must have looked much at one with the shadows.

There were two cars in front of Vic's house, both of them unfamiliar. A light-colored Ford Cortina and a Jaguar XJ 12.

I drifted round the house toward the pool, hoping and guessing that Vic used his office as I did, as the natural place to take his friends. Most of the house was in darkness. Vic's window shone with light. Round 1, I thought.

Carefully I skirted the pool and approached under the protection of the dark overhang of the roof on the guest suite, keeping tight against the wall. Faint light from the sky raised a sheen on the unruffled pool water. There was no wind, no sound except from an occasional car on the road. With caution, I edged closer.

Vic's window was hung with thick fawn-colored crusty net in clustered folds. I found that one could see a certain amount when looking through it straight ahead, but that slanting vision was impossible. It also seemed possible that as the curtaining was not opaque, anyone inside could see through it to someone moving about outside. Inconvenient for peeping Toms.

I crawled the last bit, feeling a fool. The window stretched down to within eighteen inches of the paving stones. By the time I reached the wall, I was flat on my stomach.

Vic was walking round the room, talking. I risked raising my eyes over the level of the sill, but to little purpose. All I could clearly see was a bit of the table that stood near the window, and a distant piece of Florentine mirror. I shifted sideways a little and looked again. A sliver of bookcase and a chair leg. Another shift. More bookcase, and a quick impression of Vic moving.

216

His voice came through the glass whenever he walked near the window. I put my head down and listened to unconnected snatches.

". . . Polyprint and Nestegg . . . bloody dynamite . . ."

". . . What does it matter how he found out? How did you find out in the first place? . . ."

". . . Beating him up wouldn't have worked, either. I told you . . . burning his place hurt him more. . . ."

". . . You can't put pressure on a wife and children if he hasn't got any. . . ."

". . . brother . . . no good . . . just a lush . . ."

I shifted along on my stomach and looked again. Another uninformative slice of furnishings.

I couldn't see whom Vic was talking to or hear the replies. The answering voice came to me only as a low rumble, like a bass drum played quietly. I realized in the end that its owner was sitting against the window wall but so far to the left that unless he moved I was not going to be able to see him from where I was. Never mind, I thought. I would see him face-to-face soon enough. Meanwhile I might as well learn as much as I could. There might be a gem for the bargaining session ahead.

". . . can't see any other way out . . ." Vic said.

The reply rumbled briefly.

Vic came suddenly close to the window. I buried my face and stretched my ears.

"Look," he said. "I more or less promised him you would meet him."

Rumble rumble, seemingly displeased.

"Well, I'm damn well not going inside just to save him from knowing who you are."

Rumble rumble.

"Damn right I'll tell him."

Rumble rumble rumble.

Vic hadn't been exactly frank, I thought. He hadn't told his rumble-voiced friend that I was due there at six o'clock. Vic was going to hand the friend to me on a plate whether the friend liked it or not. I smiled in the dark. Round 2.

"I don't give a damn about your reputation," Vic said. "What's so bloody marvelous about your reputation?"

A long rumble. Infuriating not to be able to hear.

Vic's voice in reply sounded for the first time as if he were stifling doubts.

"Of course I agree that business is founded on trust. . . ."

Rumble rumble.

"Well, it's too bad, because I'm not bloody going to jail to save your reputation, and that's flat."

Rumble.

Vic moved across the window from right to left, but I could still hear him clearly.

"Where are you going?" His voice suddenly rose sharply into anxiety. "What are you doing? No—no . . . My God—wait . . ." His voice went higher and louder. "Wait!"

The last time, he screamed it. *"Wait!"*

There was a sort of cough somewhere inside the room and something heavy fell against the window. I raised my head and froze in absolute horror.

Vic was leaning back against the glass. The net curtain all around him was bright scarlet.

While I watched, he twisted on his feet and gripped hold of the curtain for support. On the front of his lilac shirt there was an irregular scarlet star.

He didn't speak. His grip slackened on the curtains. I saw his eyes for a second as he fell.

218

They were dead.

Without conscious thought, I got to my feet and sprinted round to the front of the house. It's easy enough looking back to say that it was a mad thing to do. At the time, all I thought was that Vic's murdering friend would get clean away without me seeing who he was. All I thought was that I'd set Vic up to flush out the friend, and if I didn't see who it was he would have died for nothing. The one thing I didn't think was that if the friend saw *me*, he would simply shoot me, too.

Everything happened too fast for working out probabilities.

By the time I had skirted the pool and the garden room, the engine of one of the cars in the drive was urgently revving. Not the big Jaguar. The Cortina. It reversed fiercely in an arc to point its nose to the drive.

I ran. I came up to it from behind and on its left side. Inside the car the dark bulk of the driver was shifting the gears from reverse to forward. I put my hand on the handle of the rear door, wanting to open it, to make him turn his head, to see who he was, to stop him, fight him, take his gun away, hand him over to justice . . . heaven knows.

The Cortina spurted forward as it flagged off the grid and pulled my arm right out of its socket.

16

£

I knelt on the ground in the familiar bloody agony and thought that a dislocated shoulder was among the ultimates.

What was more, there were footsteps coming up the drive toward me.

Scrunch scrunch scrunch.

Inexorable.

All the things have to be faced. I supported my left elbow in my right hand and waited, because in any case I could barely move, let alone run away.

A figure materialized from the darkness. Advanced to within six feet. Stopped.

A voice said, "Have you been run over?"

I nearly smiled. "I thought I told you to stay in the car."

"You sound funny," Sophie said.

"Hilarious."

She took two paces forward, stretching out her hands.

"Don't touch me," I said hastily.

"What's the matter?"

I told her.

"Oh, God," she said.

"And you can put it back."

"What?"

"Put my shoulder back."

"But . . ." She sounded bewildered. "I can't."

"Not here. In the house."

She had no idea how to help me up. Not like jump-jockeys' wives, I thought briefly, for whom smashed-up husbands were all in the day's work. I made it to my feet with the loss of no more than a pint of sweat. Various adjectives occurred to me. Like excruciating.

One foot gingerly in front of the other took us to the door that Vic's friend had left open, the door to the hallway and the office. Light spilled out of it. I wondered if there was a telephone anywhere except in the office.

We went very slowly indoors with me hunched like Quasimodo.

"Jonah!" Sophie said.

"What?"

"I didn't realize. . . . You look—you look—"

"Yeah," I said. "I need you to put it back."

"We must get a doctor."

"No . . . the police. Vic Vincent's been shot."

"*Shot.*" She followed my gaze to Vic's office and went along there to take a look. She returned several shades paler, which made two of us.

"It's . . . awful."

"See if you can find another telephone."

She switched on several lights. There was another telephone on a table flanked by a sofa and a potted palm.

"Call the police," I said.

She dialed three nines. Told them a man had been killed. They would come at once, they said. She put the receiver down and turned toward me purposefully.

"I'm going to dial again for an ambulance."

"No. You do it. It has to be done now. At once."

"Jonah . . . don't be stupid. How can I? You need professional help. A doctor."

"I need a doctor like yesterday's news. Look, doctors don't put shoulders back. By the time they arrive, all the muscles have gone into spasms, so they can't. They send you to hospital in bloody jerking ambulances. The hospitals sit you around for hours in casualty departments. Then they send you for X-rays. Then they trundle you to an operating theatre, and by then they have to give you a general anesthetic. It takes about four hours at the best of times. Sunday evenings are not the best of times. If you won't do it, I—I—" I stopped. The prospect of those long hours ahead was enough to scare the saints.

"I can't," she said.

"I'll tell you how."

She was appalled. "You must have a doctor."

I muttered under my breath.

"What did you say?" she demanded.

"I said . . . 'God give me a woman of strength.' "

She said in a low voice, "That's unfair."

I went slowly past her through the hall into the open-plan

dining room and sat gingerly on one of the hard straight-backed chairs. What I felt was beyond a joke.

I shut my eyes and thought about Vic's friend. Thought about the glimpse of him I'd had in the split second before he blasted off and took my comfort with him. There had been a seepage of light from the house's open door. Enough to show me the shape of a head.

There are been little time for certainty. Only for impression. The impression remained in my mind indelibly.

Sophie said, "Jonah."

I opened my eyes. She was standing in front of me, huge-eyed and trembling.

I'd wanted to know what could break up her colossal composure. Now I knew. One man shot to death and another demanding an unimaginable service.

"What do I do?" she said.

I swallowed. "It will take ten minutes."

She was shocked. Apprehension made her eyes even bigger.

"If you mean it," I said.

"I do."

"First instruction . . . smile."

"But . . ."

"Six deep breaths and a big smile."

"Oh, Jonah." She sounded despairing.

"Look," I said. "I don't want you messing about with my precious body unless you go back to being your normal confident relaxed efficient hard-hearted self."

She stared. "I thought you were past talking. You're a fraud."

"That's better."

She took me literally. Six deep breaths and a smile. Not a big smile, but something.

"O.K.," I said. "Put your left hand under my elbow and hold my wrist with your right."

I shifted an inch or two back on the seat until the base of my spine was firmly against the chair back. She very tentatively stepped close in front of me and put her hands where I'd said. For all her efforts, I could see she still did not believe she could help.

"Look . . . do it slowly. You can't wrench it back. When you get my arm in the right position, the top of the bone will slide back into the socket. . . . Do you understand?"

"I think so."

"Right. . . . There are three stages. First, straighten my arm out, slightly to the side. Then keep my wrist out and pull my elbow across my chest. . . . It will look awkward, but it works. If you pull hard enough, the top of the bone will come in line with the socket and start to slide into it. When it does that, fold my wrist up and over towards my right shoulder . . . and my arm will go back where it ought to be."

She was in no way reassured.

"Sophie."

"Yes?"

I hesitated. "If you do it, you'll save me hours of pain."

"Yes."

"But—" I stopped.

"You're trying to say," she said, "that I'm going to hurt you, even worse, and I mustn't let it stop me."

"Atta girl."

"All right."

She began. Straightened my arm out, slowly and carefully.

I could feel her surprise at the physical effort it demanded of her: an arm was a good deal heavier than most people realized and she had the whole weight of it in her hands.

It took five minutes.

"Is that right?" she said.

"Mm."

"Now do I pull your elbow across?"

"Mm."

Always the worst part. When she'd gone only a short way, I could feel her trembling. Her fingers under my elbow shook with irresolution.

I said, "If you . . . drop my elbow . . . now . . . I'll scream."

"Oh . . ." She sounded shattered but her grip tightened blessedly. We proceeded, with no sound but heavy breathing on both sides. There was always a point at which progress seemed to end and yet the arm was still out. Always a point of despair.

We reached it.

"It's no good," she said. "It isn't working."

"Go on."

"I can't do it."

"Another . . . half-inch."

"Oh, no. . . ." But she screwed up her courage and went on trying.

The jolt and the audible scrunch when the bone started to go over the edge of the socket astounded her.

"Now," I said. "Wrist up and over . . . not too fast."

Two more horrible crunches, the sweetest sounds on earth. Hell went back into its box. I stood up. Smiled like the sun coming out.

"That's it," I said. "Thank you very much."

She was bewildered. "Do you mean the pain goes away just like that?"

"Just like that."

She looked at the transformation she'd wrought in me. Her eyes filled with tears. I put my right arm round her and held her close.

"Why don't you get the bloody thing fixed?" she said.

"You won't catch me having any more orthopedic operations if I don't absolutely have to."

She sniffed the tears away. "You're a coward."

"All the way."

I walked with her to Vic's office. We stood in the doorway, looking in. He lay by the window, face down, the back of his purple shirt a glistening crimson obscenity.

Whatever he had done to me, I had done worse to him. Because of the pressure I'd put on him, he was dead. I supposed I would never outlive a tormenting sense of responsibility and regret.

"I half saw who killed him," I said.

"Half?"

"Enough."

The indelible impression made sense. The pattern had become plain.

We turned away.

There was a sound of a car drawing up outside, doors slamming, two or three pairs of heavy feet.

"The police," Sophie said in relief.

I nodded. "Keep it simple, though. If they start on Vic's and my disagreements, we'll be here all night."

"You're immoral."

"No . . . lazy."

"I've noticed."

The police were their usual abrasive selves, saving their store of sympathy for worthier causes like old ladies and lost kids. They looked into the office, telephoned for reinforcements, and invited us in a fairly hectoring manner to explain what we were doing there. I stifled an irritated impulse to point out that if we'd chosen we could have gone quietly away and left someone else to find Vic dead. Virtue's own reward was seldom worth it.

Both then and later, when the higher ranks arrived, we gave minimum information and kept quiet in between. In essence I said, "There were no lights on in the front of the house when I arrived. I know the house slightly. I walked round to the side to see if Vic was in his office. I had a tentative arrangement to see him for a few minutes at six o'clock. I was driving Miss Randolph home to Esher and called in at Vic's on the way, parked outside on the road and walked up the drive. I saw him in his office. I saw him fall against the window, and then collapse. I hurried round to the front to try to get into the house to help him. A light-colored Ford Cortina was starting up. It shot away in a hurry but I caught a glimpse of the driver. I recognized the driver."

They listened to my identification impassively, neither pleased nor skeptical. Did I see a gun? they asked. There was no gun in Vic's office.

"No," I said. "Nothing but the driver's head."

They grunted and turned to Sophie.

"Jonah left me in his car," she said. "Then this other car came crashing out of the drive at a reckless speed. I decided to see if everything was all right. I walked up here and found Jonah in front of the house. The house door was open, so we went inside. We found Mr. Vincent lying in his office. We telephoned immediately to you."

We sat for nearly three hours in Vic's beautiful dining room while the end of his life was dissected by the prosaic professionals for whom murder was all in the day's work. They switched on every light and brought more of their own, and the glare further dehumanized their host.

Maybe it was necessary for them to think of him as a thing, not a person. I still couldn't.

I was finally allowed to take Sophie home. I parked outside and we went up to her flat, subdued and depressed. She made coffee, which we drank in the kitchen.

"Hungry?" she said. "There's some cheese, I think."

We ate chunks of cheese in our fingers, absent-mindedly.

"What are you going to do?" she said.

"Wait for them to catch him, I suppose."

"He won't run. . . . He doesn't know you saw him."

"No."

She said anxiously, "He doesn't . . . does he?"

"If he'd seen me, he'd have come back and shot us both."

"You think the nicest thoughts."

The evening had left smudgy circles round her eyes. She looked more than tired: overstretched, overstrained. I yawned and said I ought to be going home, and she couldn't disguise her flooding relief.

I smiled. "You'll be all right alone?"

"Oh, yes." Absolute certainty in her voice. Solitude offered her refuge, healing, and rest. I didn't. I had brought her a car crash, a man with a pitchfork, a bone-setting, and a murder. I'd offered an alcoholic brother, a half-burnt home, and a snap engagement. None of it designed for the well-being of someone who needed the order and peace of an ivory control tower.

She came with me down to the car.

"You'll come again?" she said.

"When you're ready."

"A dose of Dereham every week—"

"Would be enough to frighten any woman?"

"Well, no." She smiled. "It might be bad for the nerves, but at least I'd know I was alive."

I laughed and gave her an undemanding brotherly kiss. "It would suit me fine."

"Really?"

"And truly."

"I don't ask for that," she said.

"Then you damn well should."

She grinned. I slid into the driving seat. Her eyes looked calmer in her exhausted face.

"Sleep well," I said. "I'll call you tomorrow."

It seemed a long way home. My shoulder ached: a faint echo, but persistent. I thought with longing of a stiff brandy and stifled a sigh at the less reviving prospect of Coke.

When I got back, the house was dark.

No lights, no Crispin.

Hell, I thought. He had no car any more, no transport but his feet. The one place his feet could be trusted to take him was straight to the source of gin.

I parked outside the kitchen as usual, opened the unlocked back door, went in, switched on the lights, and shouted through the house.

"Crispin?" No answer. "Crispin."

Total silence.

Swearing under my breath, I went along to the office, intending to telephone the pub to ask what state he was in. If he was too far gone, I'd drive up and fetch him. I had picked up the receiver and begun to dial when I heard the door behind me squeak on its hinges.

So he hadn't gone after all. I turned with the beginnings of a congratulatory smile.

It wasn't Crispin who had come in. I looked at the heavy pistol with its elongated silencer, and, like Vic, the urgent words that shaped in my mind were "No" and "My God" and "Wait."

17

"Put the telephone down," he said.

I looked at the receiver in my hand. I'd dialed only half the number. Pity. I did as he said.

"I saw you at Vic's," I said. "I told the police."

The gun merely wavered a fraction. The round black hole still faced my heart. I'd seen what it had made of Vic, and I had no illusions.

"I guessed you were there," he said.

"How?"

"A car parked by the hedge . . . Saw it when I left. About twelve miles on, I realized it was yours. I went back. . . . The place was crawling with police."

My tongue felt huge and sluggish. I looked at the gun and could think of nothing useful to say.

"You and Vic," he said. "You thought you had me in a corner. Too bad. Your mistake."

I swallowed with difficulty. "I saw you," I repeated, "and the police know."

"Maybe. But they'll have trouble making it stick when you're not alive to give evidence."

I looked desperately around for a way of diverting him. For a weapon to attack him with.

He smiled faintly. "It's no good, Jonah. It's the end of the road."

He straightened his arm to the firing position adopted by people who know what they are about.

"You won't feel much," he said.

The door behind him swung on its hinges while he was already beginning to squeeze the trigger. The sudden shift of my attention from sick fascination at the round hole from which death was coming to a point behind his back was just enough to jerk his hand.

Enough was enough.

The flame spat out and the bullet missed me.

Crispin stood in the doorway looking with horror at the scene. In one hand he waved a heavy green bottle of gin.

"The old heave-ho," he said distinctly.

He wasn't drunk, I thought incredulously. He was telling me to go right back to a rugger tackle we'd perfected in boyhood. Instinctively, faster than thought, I feinted at our visitor's knees.

The gun came round and down toward me, and Crispin hit him hard on the head with the gin bottle.

The pistol swung away from me and fired, and I snapped

up and lifted the only heavy object within reach, which was my typewriter. I crashed it down with all my strength in the wake of the gin bottle, and the visitor sprawled on the floor with blood gushing from his scalp and the typewriter ribbon rolling across his unconscious face and away to the wall.

"You old crazy loon," I said breathlessly, turning to Crispin. "You old blessed . . ."

My voice died away. Crispin half sat, half lay on the floor with his hand pressed to his side.

"Crispin!"

"I'm . . . not . . . drunk," he said.

"Of course not."

"I think . . . he shot me."

Speechlessly I knelt beside him.

He said, "Was he the one . . . who burnt the yard?"

"Yes."

"Hope . . . you killed him."

His body sagged. I caught him. Eased him down to the floor and with one hand grabbed a cushion for his head. His pressing fingers relaxed and fell away, and there on the waistband of his trousers was the spreading patch of blood.

"I'm . . . floating," he said. He smiled. "It's better . . . than . . . being drunk."

"I'll get a doctor," I said.

"No . . . Jonah . . . Don't leave me . . . you sod."

I didn't leave him. Three minutes later, without speaking again, he left me.

I closed his eyes gently and got stiffly to my feet, trying to fold numbness around me like a coat.

The pistol lay where it had fallen. I pushed it carefully with my toe until it was completely out of sight under the low-slung armchair. I didn't want the visitor waking to grab it again.

The visitor hadn't moved. I sat on the edge of my desk and looked down at the two of them, the unconscious and the dead.

Time enough, I thought, to call in those more or less constant companions, the busy and probing police. A quarter of an hour sooner or later, what did it matter? There was nothing any more to be gained. Too much had been irrevocably lost.

I didn't care how much damage I'd done with the typewriter. The head I'd busted with it looked more bloody than dented, but I felt a strong aversion to exploring. In all my life I had never wanted to kill anyone; had never thought I could come within a mile of it. I had not even intended to kill with the typewriter, but only to stun. I sat quietly on the desk and shook with fury inside, and wished I could have that blow back again, so that I could make it heavier, avenging and fatal.

Whatever my brother had been, he had been my brother. No one had the right to kill him. I think at that moment I felt as primitive as the Sicilians.

From greed, the visitor had set out to destroy me. Not because I'd done him any harm. Simply because I stood in his plundering way. He'd sent me a message; join or be flattened, an ultimatum as old as tyranny.

My own fault, as they had tirelessly pointed out, if the answer I'd chosen was flatten and be damned.

Kerry Sanders had been only a convenient means. Had she not thought of her equine birthday present, another way would have been found. The intention was the activating force. The means were accidental.

I remembered what Pauli Teksa had said at dinner that evening at Newmarket. I remembered his exact words. The classic law of the invader was to single out the strongest guy around and smash him, so that the weaker crowd would come to heel like lambs.

At various times I had thought of the man who lay on my carpet as "someone," as the expert, as Vic's friend, as the driver, and as the visitor; Pauli's word—the invader—suited him best.

He had invaded the bloodstock game with gangster ethics. Invaded Vic's life and business as a dangerous ally. Invaded mine as a destroyer.

The fact that I did not feel that I filled the role he'd cast me in had not mattered. It was the invader's view that had mattered. My bad luck that he'd seen me as the strongest guy around.

There was no way of winning against a determined invader. If you gave in at once, you lost. If you fought to the death, you still lost, even if you won. The price of victory was sore.

Pauli Teksa had said, just before he went back to America, that it was easier to start things than to stop them. He had been warning me that if I lashed back at Vic I could find myself in even more trouble than before.

He had been right.

But he had been speaking also of himself.

Pauli Teksa, the invader, lay face down on my carpet, my broken typewriter beside his bloody head.

The stocky tough wide-shouldered body looked a solid hunk of bull muscle. The crinkly black hair was matted and running with red. I could see half of his face: the strong distinctive profile with the firm mouth now slackly open, the swift eye shut.

His hands lay loosely on the floor, one each side of his head. He wore two thick gold rings. A gold-and-platinum wristwatch. Heavy gold cuff links. The tip of the gold mountain he had siphoned off through Vic.

I thought it likely that his British venture had been an extension of activities at home. The super-aggressive kickback operation had been too polished to be a trial run. Maybe he had set up Vic-equivalents in other countries. Maybe Vics in South America and Italy and Japan were rooking the local Constantines and Wilton Youngs for him and driving the Antonia Huntercombes to despair.

Vic and Fynedale had been amateurs, compared with him. Fynedale working himself into a white murdering manic state. Vic nearing apoplexy with easy rage. Pauli stayed cool and used his eyes and made his snap decisions, and when he saw the need to kill he did it without histrionics. An unfortunate necessity, best done quickly.

He had even, with macabre kindness, told me I wouldn't feel much, and I believed him. I'd heard shot people say all they had felt was a sort of thud, and hadn't realized they were wounded until afterward. If you were shot through the heart, there was no afterward, and that was that.

He had himself urged me several times to throw in my lot with Vic, and go along with the crowd. He'd warned me of the dangers of holding out. He'd given me the advice as a friend, and behind the smile there had been an enemy as cold as bureaucracy.

I realized slowly that perhaps at one point he had in fact done his best to stop what he'd started. He had said no to some demand of Vic's, and he had gone home to America. But by then it was too late, because in burning my stable he had switched me from tolerance to retaliation. Bash me, I bash back. The way wars started, big and small.

On the floor, Pauli stirred.

Not dead.

Across the room, the gin bottle lay where Crispin had dropped it. I shoved myself off the desk and went over to pick it up. If Pauli were to return to consciousness, groggy or not, I'd trust him as far as I could throw the Empire State Building. A reinforcing clunk with green glass would be merely prudent.

I looked closer at the bottle. It was full. In addition the seal was unbroken.

I returned to the desk and set the bottle on it, and looked down with impossible grief at my brother. I knew that I had needed him as much as he needed me. He was at the roots of my life.

Pauli stirred again. The urge to finish off what I'd started was almost overwhelming. No one would know. No one could tell whether he'd been hit twice or three times. Killing someone who was trying to kill you was justifiable in law, and who was to guess that I'd killed him ten minutes later?

The moment passed. I felt cold suddenly, and old and lonely and as tired as dust. I stretched out a hand to the telephone, to call the cops.

It rang before I touched it. I picked up the receiver and said dully, "Hello?"

"Mr. Crispin Dereham?" A man's voice, educated.

"I'm his brother," I said.

"Could I speak to him?"

237

"I'm afraid," I said, "he's . . . unavailable."

"Oh, dear." The voice sounded warmly sympathetic. "Well, this is Alcoholics Anonymous. Your brother telephoned us earlier this evening asking for help, and we promised to ring him back again for another chat. . . ."

He went on talking for some time, but I didn't hear a word he said.

Race to finish the complete list of

DICK FRANCIS

national bestsellers published by Fawcett Books.

BANKER
Young investment banker Tim Ekaterin has decided to join the exciting world of horse racing. When the multi-million dollar loan he arranges to finance the purchase of Sandcastle, a champion, is threatened by an apparent defect in the horse, Tim searches desperately for an answer. Violence and murder do not deter him.

BLOOD SPORT
When English agent Gene Hawkins agreed to search for millionaire Dave Teller's prized missing stallion, he didn't know his retainer would include the attention of his boss's beautiful teenage daughter—or Teller's seldom sober wife. He also didn't know that his search would lead to murder.

BOLT
In Kit Fielding's breakneck world of steeplechase racing, the ultimate catastrophe strikes. Someone is shooting the horses with a weapon fiendishly called a "humane killer." Kit must stop the murdering madness, and everyone in his upper-crust circle becomes a suspect.

BONECRACK
Neil Griffon has no choice—a no-compromise crime czar gives him an ultimatum that he dare not refuse. The czar's son must be hired by Griffon's stable to ride in the Derby. And his son must be trained to win or Griffon's very life will be lost.

BREAK IN
Kit Fielding, proud heir to tradition and sporting hero to legions of fans, is drawn into a crusade to save his twin sister's marriage from ruinous scandal. His intercession proves more costly than he'd imagined by thrusting him into a deadly contest with a ruthless media czar, a black-hearted robber baron, and a violent adversary far too close to home for comfort.

COMEBACK
When globe-hopping British First Secretary Peter Darwin returns to his childhood home of Glouscestershire, England, he must confront long-hidden memories, a string of racehorse deaths, and homicide. Darwin soon realizes that the key to the dark events involves his own past, and he soon wishes he'd never come back, because he just might never leave again . . . alive.

THE DANGER
Kidnapping is Andrew Douglas's business. They take them, he finds them. But it isn't so simple when Alessia Cenci, golden-girl jockey, disappears, followed by the young child of a Derby winner and the senior steward of the Jockey Club. Andrew's caseload is suddenly, violently overflowing.

DEAD CERT
As he rode through the thick English fog, jockey Alan York was looking at an all-too-familiar sight; the back of champion rider Bill Davidson astride the great racehorse Admiral. But this was one race York was destined to win. Before Admiral jumped the last fence, Bill Davidson would be dead. Alan knew racing was a dangerous sport, but he also knew this was no accident.

THE EDGE
The Great Transcontinental Mystery Race is a rail junket that offers passengers the chance to race thoroughbreds and to solve mysteries. For Tor Kelsey, undercover agent for the British Jockey Club, this imaginary mayhem is about to become a nightmare of real murder.

ENQUIRY

Jockey Kelly Hughes and trainer Dexter Cranfield are charged with throwing a race for personal profit and are barred from racing—a devastating event for them both. It is a vicious frame-up, and Hughes refuses to take the phony verdict lying down—even though his personal enquiry might have him lying down permanently.

FLYING FINISH

According to just about everybody, Henry Grey had a bad disposition. But Henry knew all he needed was a new job. The air transport of racehorses would let him see the world and maybe change his luck. His luck changed all right—when he found there was something more than horseflesh in the cargo hold.

FORFEIT

James Tyrone, racing reporter, knew that fellow writer Bert Chekov was a drunk. When Bert died in an "accidental" fall from a window, Tyrone suspected that Bert's death might be related to some columns he'd written touting can't-lose horses that failed to show up on race day. Tyrone vowed to prove that Chekov was murdered, despite the terrifying risk involved.

FOR KICKS

Daniel Roke couldn't leave his Australian stud farm to look into an English horse-doping scandal. Or so he said. But soon he was in England taking over investigative duties vacated by a racing journalist who had died in an "auto accident." Then Daniel learned that men who would give drugs to horses would do much worse to human beings.

HIGH STAKES

Steven Scott is a novice horse owner who is having an incredible string of luck at the races. He uncovers deceit in his own stables and gets rid of the troublemaker, only to find that he himself is marked for murder.

HOT MONEY
With five ex-wives and nine children, wealthy gold trader Malcolm Pembroke presides over a motley clan in constant conflict with one another. When Malcolm's least likable ex-wife dies violently, he calls on his son, Ian, the family jockey, to protect him from their nearest, if not always dearest, relatives. Ian must delve into the dark Pembroke past that simmers with greed, hate, and vengefulness to uncover what could motivate blood to strike against blood.

IN THE FRAME
Charles Todd is an artist who must figure out a masterpiece of murder and thereby clear his cousin's name. Todd finds himself involved in a dangerous manhunt for a brilliant and elusive killer.

LONGSHOT
John Kendall, writer of travel guides, is impulsive, but taking an assignment because he needs money hardly seems a rash act. Off to rural England Kendall goes to interview a successful racehorse trainer. Soon Kendall realizes that the perils described in his survival manuals pale next to the dangers in rural England. "Impulse will kill you one of these days," his agent had warned. Kendall should have listened, but he didn't—not by a longshot.

NERVE
Rob Finn was a misfit—a struggling jockey in a family of musicians, a man in love with a beautiful woman who wouldn't have him, a rider who—just as it seemed he was breaking into racing's big time—lost his nerve. Or did he? The horses felt too sluggish beneath him, and he knew there had to be a reason. When he found it, he could barely believe it. And when it found him, he could barely breathe.

ODDS AGAINST
Ex-jockey Sid Halley had a wrecked hand, a mean case of depression, and a need for a new career. He joined a detective agency, took a bullet in his side, and was sent out on a case of his own. Then he met Zanna Martin, a woman who could make life worth living again. But it was an even-money bet that he'd be killed before he had a chance to start over.

PROOF
Wine merchant Tony Beach finds himself caught in the midst of a terrifying mystery beginning with sham scotch and counterfeit claret and escalating to hijacking and murder. Tony must draw on every reserve of hidden courage to crack a sophisticated scam and to save many lives including his own.

RAT RACE
Matt Shore is flying some racing fans to the track when he is forced to make an emergency landing minutes before the plane blows up. And this is only the beginning, as Matt is caught up in a flurry of secrets, schemes, and sudden violence that puts him on the wrong side of the odds.

REFLEX
Jockey Philip Nore is no ordinary hero. When he suspects that a track photographer's fatal accident was really murder, he sets out to discover the truth and to trap the killer. Slowly, he unravels some nasty secrets of corruption, blackmail, and murder, and unwittingly sets himself up as the killer's next target.

SLAY RIDE
British investigator David Cleveland comes to Norway in search of Robert Sherman, a champion jockey who had disappeared right before the Norwegian National—a race he was certain to win. Cleveland is sure that Sherman's disappearance is tied to a gruesome string of deaths that he soon finds are meant to include his own.

SMOKESCREEN
Edward Lincoln, star of the silver screen, journeys to South Africa to rescue his ailing godmother, Nerissa. Nerissa asks Edward to save her racehorses, but Edward discovers a plot for murder—human murder. Edward must give the performance of his life to find a killer.

STRAIGHT
"I inherited my brother's life and it nearly killed me." So says Derek Franklin, an injured steeplechase jockey, who must try to untangle his brother's complex life—filled with women, precious gems, and horses—without losing his own.

TRIAL RUN
It seems the Prince's brother-in-law has his heart set on riding in the Olympics, but a jealous Russian has her heart set on killing him if he does. So Randall Drew leaves his well-bred horses and high-born girlfriend and goes to Moscow. He does not expect the sabotage and murder he finds there, nor the unspeakable terror that follows.

TWICE SHY
Young physicist Jonathan Derry is given some musical tapes by a friend. But the tapes are really an elaborate computerized horse betting system that can make the owner a rich man—or a dead one.

WHIP HAND
No longer able to jockey, Sid Halley has become quite a good private eye, though he is haunted by memories of his past glories. When the wife of one of England's top trainers comes to beg for help in preventing some foul play at the track, Sid Halley begins to know what being haunted really means.

DICK FRANCIS